REIGN

UNDERWORLD KINGS BOOK IV

LILAH LANCE

To the girl who said I will rise or raise hell

AUTHOR'S NOTE

This is the final book in the Underworld Kings.

While this book can be read as a standalone, it would be helpful not mandatory to read the previous three books before this.

CONTENT WARNING

This book contains:

- A morally gray Alpha-male
- Mature themes
- Explicit content
- Mentions of assault/sexual assault
- Graphic Language
- Mentions of human trafficking/kidnapping
- Violence

FIVE YEARS AGO

1

VIVIANNE

"You don't look so good, everything straight?"

I walked up to Mamie—my grandmother, in bed reading a historical romance novel.

The same ones that I tried to sneak and read over my teenage years despite not really understanding anything about it.

Mamie was hitting her seventies and she shouldn't be working so hard.

But my little brother Erik and I were teenagers still and I couldn't fucking wait until I turned eighteen to take care of Mamie.

Right now she was lying in her bed with her romance novel, when I walked in from school.

"Hey there darlin'," she sat up slowly and even I noticed how she struggled. "Where's Erik?"

"He's at some afterschool program for some specialized college. Erik's looking to go and be a doctor."

"Ever since he was in diapers," she laughed hiding a cough into her elbow.

My brother was fifteen, looking at Kingston Prep in New York, a private college that was known for giving out full rides to those who wanted it.

Part of why it was so attractive as a whole.

I just fucking hoped Erik got one.

I was not as smart as Erik. All of my plans were maybe one year out.

I was dropping out in another year when I turned eighteen so I could work full time for Mamie and Erik.

Sure, even if I was a cashier at a grocery store, I wouldn't make much, but it would be enough for Mamie to live off retirement. She'd been taking care of us for so long.

After my Mama was caught with drugs and my father died, Mamie took in me and Erik at a young age.

I remember being nine and her picking me up, taking one look at my dirty clothes and Erik and us never going back.

Since then, she'd been my entire world.

Even now I saw that spirit in her eyes. She didn't know where her daughter had gone wrong, but it was clear Mama wasn't in the right state of mind to take care of us.

Now? Seeing her in her bedroom, in the pale yellow walls of our rundown apartment, I didn't like the look in her eyes or the watery smile she gave me.

"You good?" I asked her as she brushed my raven-hair back.

I wanted to dye it flaming red like Mamie's so my freckles wouldn't be too much for my face, but I didn't.

Mamie forbid me from dying my hair to not ruin it.

"I'm tired," she breathed out easily. "That's all. Normal stuff as an adults, you know?"

I did know. I felt guilty my entire teenage years watching Mamie put food on the table so I did what I could.

When I went grocery shopping with her, I always scanned items wrong to be cheaper, I always switched price tags or used my little fingers to grab more food than necessary for Erik and Mamie.

Was it stealing?

Sure.

But we were piss poor broke, in a shit neighborhood, and I had no idea how I was going to get myself out. Enlist in the military?

Mamie forbid it.

Don't need you fighting another man's fight.

"So you feel good?" I checked in.

2

Mamie nodded. "You and Erik need to study to make sure you both can go away to college."

I smiled knowing full well I wasn't making it to college. At all. But she didn't have to know that.

I puffed out a breath. "Come on, I got us some sandwiches for dinner."

"You got us some?" She frowned disapprovingly.

"Yeah, food waste, plenty of it in the city."

Chicago was known for being shit in some areas. Better in others.

We happen to get hand me downs from private schools all the time. Part of the reason why I had Mamie switch us to this school.

Turns out, it had a pipeline into a better school.

One Erik wanted to go to but we couldn't afford it.

At our school though, they gave away these free meals inside coolers with turkey and cheese sandwiches, a bag of carrots, and some milk. Going hungry at home meant carrying six of them in my bag.

Splitting it with my family when I got home.

Reality for me was a little different from everyone else.

"Come on, I got plenty, you don't gotta worry about dinner tonight."

She frowned. "You don't gotta do all that, Emmy."

"It's all good, come on. You're getting old," I teased.

I loved Mamie like nothing else in this world. She had saved my life and Erik's from a shit situation with Mama.

And even if I loved and missed Mama, Mamie was the one who chose us. Who saved two dirty kids, I would do anything for her.

I had set everything out in the kitchen for her and we walked by the enormous artwork in the living room Mamie had hung up since we moved here.

Storm by some French artist. A complete fucking knock-off painting Mamie had for centuries in her family.

"How'd your day go?" I asked her as we fell into an easy routine.

"Vivianne ," she smiled over at me at all the food. "Promise me something."

"Yeah, anything."

3

"You know where my cards and everything are right?"

I did. I always knew. And I knew she hid extra money in a biscuit tin under her bed. Old school.

I told her that and she laughed. "Good, if you ever need it, don't be shy, honeybun. Just take some."

"Nah, I'm straight, Mamie. I promise. They feed the fuck out of us at school," I grinned. "Private school kids will shit on anything they eat, so we get scraps."

She shook her head ruefully. "If you went to that private school you'd be better off."

"And fight every single day with some rich bitch for my seat? I'm straight, come on, pass me a sandwich."

I did get a scholarship to go to the private school.

I didn't tell Mamie.

During a summer program I had gone there and I got made fun of for wearing the same clothes.

One of the girls in particular had counted all of my outfits that I had worn and ganged up on me during morning recess.

You've worn the same shirt in the last week.

You can't wear the same clothes in the same month.

I didn't know that. I didn't know there were invisible class rules to exist in society.

What brands I needed to wear to be a chosen one to the insufferable elite.

I would never forget the experience of being around girls who felt like they were better than you because their mother was a paralegal for a celebrity or because your grandmother could only afford a few thrifted shirts.

I would never forget in the morning I sat while Mamie washed and ironed every single piece of my clothes so I would have nice clothes to wear.

Watching some stupid bitch named Jenny and her crones tell me I couldn't wear it? It wasn't an insult to me but to Mamie.

So I stopped the summer program telling Mamie I was more annoyed than anything else by those girls.

Disappointed was more like it.

I didn't think they understood even if they were from better off families?

We were all there on a scholarship program.

But those girls wanted to out-rich each other.

Even if I got the summer program scholarship, the idiotic kids being raised by their vapid parents made it harder for me on every single aspect.

So I went back to public school and found I felt better around kids who wore the same hoodie every single day.

Not everyone could afford lobster and fancy Italian spaghetti.

Maybe I was a turkey and cheese kinda girl anyway. And that wasn't a bad thing to be.

"One day, I'm gonna make a lot of money," I muttered knowing Mamie was listening.

I felt the stinging in my eyes as I said it.

"I'm gonna come home and you and Erik are gonna eat good shit and I'm never gonna worry about money again."

Mamie grinned at me. "Keep dreaming, honeybun. You'll get there."

2

<hr>

VIVIANNE

"Mamie, Erik and I are leaving!"

I kicked on her door and then ran out with Erik one morning.

I thought nothing of it.

"You gonna be good at school today?" Erik asked me adjusting his glasses. My brother was almost blind. Almost.

His raven-hair hair falling over his eyes. His too skinny legs in jeans and a hoodie, but his smile was wide.

Erik and I never fought much. Maybe because we both understood the importance of what our situation was and we'd never let it get to us.

Or maybe because we knew better.

Two peas in a pod.

"Yeah," I walked with him to the bus stop, the colder Chicago air sinking into my skin. "It's always so fucking cold here."

"Hm, we need jacket," Erik said. "Look, I was thinking we might go thrifting this year and find some. Heard some rich folk drop off their stuff at that thrift store down on Main?"

"Yeah, we can do that," I said as I passed by Greenie on his stoop of the apartment building. Everyone knew Greenie. He was a gangbanger of a sort. Not quite or out. Just existing.

In a white t-shirt and socks in his sandals. Nobody knew his last name or where he came from. He was between twenty and forty. And I couldn't ever tell anything about him.

I just knew whenever shit hit the fan ever—Mamie called Greenie to deal with our greedy landlord. With the issues in the apartment.

Greenie was the fixer as we called it.

"Sup Greens."

"Sup. Sup little bro."

Erik grinned as we walked past him to the bus stop. Erik and I got on and found our seat and I thought nothing of anything the entire day.

Another day in high school and I sat through AP Lit and fucked off while everyone else listened diligently.

I didn't understand the big deal.

It wasn't a hard class.

Every single that about that day was normal.

By the time I cut last period and ran home from school on an earlier bus?

I knew Erik was taking his classes and I wanted to curl up in bed. I didn't want to be bothered.

The legit hit that massive painting as I knocked on Mamie's door figuring she stepped out again for something. She did her daily walk and got some groceries and walked back.

I ended up knocking on her door again and opening it to check.

"Mamie? You up?" She was laying in bed rolled over hugging her spare pillow to her and my heart cracked open. "Mamie."

Her romance novel open on the nightstand.

"Come on, let's get you up, I can get us some soup."

Legitimately if it made her feel better.

I shook her gently and she didn't move and I frowned adjusted my body so I wasn't sitting on the bed no more, just shaking her awake.

"Mamie?" I kept going. "Mamie, what's wrong?"

The sunlight still hit her from the afternoon sun and her body felt colder to the touch. I frowned even deeper.

"Mamie, what's wrong? Why won't you wake up?

My voice cracked open.

"Mamie, it's me, your honey bun."

Get Greenie.

He will know what to do. This was not a street you called the cops in. *The fixer.*

So I ran for it.

I RAN TO GREENIE'S STOOP WHERE I SAW HIM A MOMENT AGO. BUT he wasn't there. So I ran to his apartment and banged on the door.

"Greenie!"

He opened looking disheveled, smelling like weed and coffee. I couldn't ever tell where Greenie was from.

"Sup, raven—"

"I need your help—" I broke off as I quickly shoved in to his shock. "Something's wrong with Mamie. Please, help me."

I was surprised at how quickly he moved. "Show me the way."

We moved upstairs together and I did implicitly trust Greenie. I did. Only when he saw Mamie his face fell.

"Shit, raven…"

He wiped a hand down his face.

"What?"

I felt the way my gut twisted and everything I ate came up for lunch.

He turned to me. "All right, if we tell the fucking state they come and take you and Erik away. If we don't move her, either way you're fucked—"

"What are you talking about?"

My stomach twisted harder.

"What?"

"raven," he motioned to Mamie. "She's gone."

And even if it confirmed what I already knew? Hearing made me gag. I ran to our tiny bathroom upchucking everything into the toilet. I couldn't stop. Wiping my mouth after what felt like forever, I felt nauseous. Dizzy. Anxiety brewing in my stomach again.

I didn't want to eat a single thing.

"You straight, raven-hair? We gotta move—"

"My grandma just died—"

"Doesn't matter." I turned around to find Greenie watching me with a bit of sympathy and more nerves in those brown-eyes of his. "We gotta get rid of her body or we gotta call the cops."

"What?"

"If you do not call the cops? I can get rid of her—"

"Get rid of her?"

"But if you do, you lose Erik. You enter the system. Highly likely they separate you two. I don't trust nothing the government does."

The idea of losing Erik after losing Mamie was even more devastating and I felt like my heart was being ripped out.

"What...I don't..."

I shook my head and if Greenie knew I was at a loss, he didn't comment.

"I can bury her quietly," he murmured with a light shrug. "Gives you a few months to turn eighteen. Then you have custody over Erik. Solid stuff. Nobody has to know."

A thousand different questions ran through me in that moment.

About Mamie. About Erik. About money. About the apartment.

I felt it all bubbling up inside of me.

I nodded. "I can't lose Erik. But I don't want her thrown out like trash." My voice croaked as I said it and I couldn't even imagine the agony that flooded me at the idea of not being able to properly bury Mamie.

Mamie.

Grandma.

Because I didn't want to lose Erik.

It was her or him and he was all I had.

Greenie nodded. "I'll be back, look around and grab whatever cash you can of hers, you'll need it for rent and this is on the house. But if you need work? I can get that together."

I nodded frantically. "Thank you."

His smile was tight. "Don't thank me yet."

Greenie told me to make myself useful and clean the house. As in the sheets, take all the money I knew of and put it somewhere else. I knew Mamie's pin so I could continue withdrawing money from the bank from her payments she got for unemployment now.

Greenie's plan was...full of scheming but I understood there was nothing else for me to do. Mamie had paid off the rent and I held her one last time before Greenie got his friends involved.

I didn't know where they took Mamie, Greenie said it was better if I didn't know how they were going to bury her or cremate her.

I didn't know if Mamie had any dying wishes.

But I had to tell Erik.

That day Erik came home and I had done the laundry, running up and down the stairs, cleaning up the entire house, and praying nobody knew.

Greenie texted me when Mamie was "good" and I spent the evening alternating between cleaning and vomiting up everything I ate.

"Hey," I opened the door for him and he looked exhausted. "I know you got school tomorrow, but I have to talk to you about something."

"Can it wait a sec? I applied for a new summer program today for med school and I want Mamie to see it." Erik looked excited holding paperwork and his ripped backpack. I blinked back my emotion.

"Uhh, it's about Mamie."

His smile dropped. "What's wrong?"

"Uhh," I was bad at this. Really bad at it. "I came home today..." I slowly felt like I was underwater explaining it to him. "We can't tell anyone, otherwise they'll separate us, I have money..." I scrambled to explain to him the money we had, giving him some bills and splitting the rest for rent. "Greenie says—"

"You got Greenie?" He blinked wiping his eyes as he cried quietly.

But Erik and I had grown up in this neighborhood.

We both knew the way the world worked.

For people like us the world wasn't a fair place.

Or a kind one.

He nodded wiping his eyes over and over again as I told him Erik nodded every so often.

Stoic as ever, he was processing it objectively and I was so grateful to have him for a little brother.

"I can't lose you," I whispered unable to speak. "I won't."

He nodded and then before I knew what I was doing, we were both moving hugging each other and I felt myself quietly crying as he hugged me back tighter.

I didn't know how long we stayed like that. I just knew Erik was my entire world.

"I don't have to go to college," Erik muttered. "I can drop out and work with you."

"No," I pulled back fiercely wiping my eyes. "We got enough, don't worry about it."

～

WHEN ERIK WENT TO BED, I DIDN'T.

I stayed up counting the money Mamie had, finishing her laundry and not packing up her things, but my eyes landed on the romance novel on her counter. The apartment felt wrong to exist in without her.

And I hated who I was right then. Hated being seventeen. Hated being a kid.

Hated existing.

I was ashamed to be this girl. Ashamed at how powerless I felt. A slave to the money. I needed a way to keep my family together.

Any way possible.

Even if it meant cutting corners.

I didn't eat that night and I made a pile of things to donate or sell. My eyes landed on the enormous painting on the wall.

The shame hit me in waves staring at the Storm. Two lovers running across the grounds towards their home in the distance. Mamie had it for years.

It had been in her family for generations and I couldn't even think of selling it. I sat there on the couch for a long time knowing Erik had school in the morning. But I wouldn't be going to school.

Or doing anything.

Over the next few weeks, I counted my cash, drained Mamie's

bank account to be able to make rent for the next three months straight with some groceries.

I could go to food pantries so I spent my time locating those.

The most expensive thing for me was period products, so I found if I got on birth control at the local free clinics?

It was cheaper to not get a period. With one less concern, I went about my life.

A few weeks into me struggling to sit through classes, I saw Erik's backpack strap break again.

He needed new shoes.

His glasses frame was getting old and I saw a few kids snickering at him.

I immediately felt a wave of fury wash over me as I saw Erik's cheeks turn red. My brother was taller than me and just a kid.

He deserves better.

I need more money.

I need cash.

"Come on, kiddo, let's go home."

He nodded. Eric was a shy kid. He wouldn't say anything. But I saw how red his cheeks got as we walked out and I saw the holes on the back of his cheap sneakers.

A burning sensation filled my chest.

On the bus, I got us off a stop early.

I had sixty dollars in my pocket. It felt like a fortune.

"Where are we going?" Eric said as we walked down to a corner store owned by some Asian lady who sold knockoff shoes.

"It's a surprise."

I walked inside the tiny shop that looked like something out of a third world country store, and I went to their sneakers.

"No, sis—" Erik protested. "I don't need it—"

"Yes, you do." I was trying not to break down. "I can afford it."

I couldn't. But my shoes were better off than his.

"I can." I shut him down as I picked out some black ones. "These are black, you won't be able to tell if there's something wrong with them."

Erik chewed his lip as I carried it to the front after finding them at forty bucks. A steal.

As we checked out Erik picked out some black socks and added those shyly and I didn't say a word.

The total was fifty-five dollars.

On the way back to the bus stop, I bought us candy.

An even sixty now.

I need money from somewhere.

Erik laughed as he tried on his sneakers and ate his candy.

And for a second I felt good.

I felt like a good big sister who didn't have dreams beyond a shit bank account.

I promised Mamie I could take care of him. I didn't even go see her even though Greenie promised we'd be okay.

I just went home and sat in front of the Storm wishing to myself that Mamie's get rich quick plan of finding buried treasure one day was real.

I WENT TO GREENIE THE NEXT DAY KNOWING I WAS ONE MONTH AWAY from being fucked over. I couldn't graduate high school, and now?

I needed more.

Money. Time. Everything.

I had no more money for the fourth month and I had no fucking clue what to do.

In a few more months I would be eighteen, I could get a normal job. A normal life. A normal everything. Not this.

He was on his stoop as usual all nonchalant despite him having covered for me and what happened with Mamie. Except this time on his arm was a dark haired woman.

I couldn't ever tell what race these people were, ambiguously mixed with everything under the sun.

"I need to make money," I said without preamble ignoring her.

"How much?"

"More than enough."

He was quiet for a bit like he was exhausted and he knew I was going to come to him.

Greenie leaned back smoking his joint, the smell rising up.

"You want me to start selling?" I motioned to his weed.

"Nah, shits dangerous and only pays enough if you got the skills. Nah, you don't want that." His throat worked. "You could always do something else?"

He motioned to the raven-hair lady on the stoop with him who squinted up at me looking too thin in her too ripped up dress.

A hooker.

"You want me to do that?"

"Your call, raven." I was about to tell Greenie to fuck off. Until he said. "She makes about a grand a night."

"*What?*"

He tipped his head. "Not street corner shit. High end, classy—"

"Private clients," she looked up at me. "With a little makeup, you could do it too."

And I already knew what she was saying but it was the money. I could practically see the fridge full of food.

I didn't have to keep putting rice into the canned chicken soup I'd been reheating. Or extra beans.

Erik was growing and I *knew* he was starving.

"A grand," I muttered.

"Sometimes more," he said. "Sometimes even more. It's not the same as dealing, but it's income."

"And you don't gotta do it forever, but how old are you?" She asked me.

I told her.

She smiled. "Even better."

And so I became a high-end escort.

3

VIVIANNE

I didn't have enough money to feed Erik.

I told myself this over and over again as my hands shook while I walked to the hotel.

My reflection looking back in the black glass, in my green dress, with my new flaming red hair? Was one of a woman older than seventeen.

Older than I was feeling.

I didn't recognize myself when Greenie had introduced me to some of his "friends."

They'll get you work.

I tried submitting a resume for jobs, but nobody wanted to hire me without experience.

But I asked them if I didn't have the experience how could I get hired?

The few places I did apply to wanted me to work for free before I could work there. Which meant not at all.

I stopped going to school and instead focused on what the raven-hair girl Heather told me to do.

She said there was an enormous business in Chicago for dating older men and looking like arm candy.

I just had to look the part. Heather did that for me.

"Just drink the wine and then smile," she told me as she did my eyeliner. "Laugh at everything he says, always repeat the last line of what he says, don't touch him but let him touch you. Remember these guys are married, they wanna feel special and like they're catching something good."

I took everything she said into my mental notes.

My first client was some finance guy from San Francisco.

A silver fox as Heather said.

Tan line where his wedding ring should be. His friend was with Heather.

The first night wasn't so bad until we had to go upstairs to the guys hotel room.

It was my first time with a man and it didn't even matter to me. I just wanted the cash.

I made sure to have my first drink before I did it.

Heather told me to have lubricant on me and apply some in the bathroom since these guys didn't give a shit about us.

They don't care if you're comfortable remember this isn't about you. You're just a blow up doll to them. Act like it and they'll pay you. If he ever gets violent, he'll pay you extra as long as he doesn't kill you.

That money's the best.

I got lucky though.

His dick gave out halfway through and he sighed and wanted me to jerk him off. Which I didn't mind.

My technique was off but I learned men who paid for this kind of stuff didn't give a shit about anything. Awkward handjobs and all, he eventually got off as I made up some shit to say to him. Heather made me watch a few videos on her phone of tapes she'd made and she didn't even care.

I was adjusting and fast.

By the end of the night he was passing out and he motioned to his wallet. "Take whatever you need."

What?

I never washed my hands so quickly in my life. I didn't feel anything between my legs but I was grateful he wore a condom. In his wallet at the foot of the bed while he dozed, I stopped for a nanosecond.

Bills.

Bills.

And bills.

More bills than I'd ever seen in my life.

I didn't even think twice.

I grabbed the entire stack leaving a few in there for him. He wouldn't miss it.

I took it and moved so quickly grabbing a jacket and rushing out of there.

On the way out of the hotel I didn't know if anyone knew how wide eyed I was. How young I was.

How crazy I might look. Out on the street a hysterical laugh filled my throat as I fisted the money tightly in my hand in my pocket.

"Oh my god..." I walked by a shop selling coats and I grabbed two.

Two coats, two pairs of gloves, two hats. Jeans. Shirts. My hands overflowed.

I spent it on clothes for Erik and a backpack. I checked out and it didn't even make a dent.

I hauled it all to the curb even after the lady gave me a weird look as I set cash down.

When I got home, I found Erik passed out in his room at the desk studying. Textbooks spread under him and his light on.

I didn't want to wake him, but I set everything down and even if it was night? I couldn't calm down. I couldn't relax.

I needed to do something.

I needed to scream.

I ran to my room and quickly threw on some sweats and then rushed back outside to the grocery store two blocks down and this late? Nobody was there.

Grabbing whatever I could? I paid at the front not knowing what was in the cart.

Milk, eggs, cheese, bread, chocolate, and everything else in between.

Thank fuck for twenty-four hour shops. I ran home with that

and once the fridge was stocked, the cabinets full of whatever we needed—I felt calm again.

I scrubbed every inch of that motherfucker off me and fell into the couch looking at the painting of the Storm.

"Not too shabby, huh?" I laid out my money counting it.

But even with the amount I had? I had enough just to make rent. Once we ran out of food? We'd be back at it.

So I was going to have to take on a new job.

So I did.

ERIK THOUGHT GREENIE GOT US ALL THE NICE THINGS, BUT I TOLD him I found some money leftover Mamie left us.

And I began doing jobs with Heather.

Some were okay. Some were fine. Some were unpleasant.

Men as it turned out needed company too.

The married men were the best. You could be whoever they wanted to be for a night and you just had to listen to them. They didn't care how old I was on paper.

I looked young, but they loved that.

"The younger you look, the better," Heather said fixing my hair up into pigtails. "They pay extra if you pretend to be their step-daughter."

And so I did.

I took home money. *MONEY*.

Suddenly, I was measuring my life in rent and the ability to help Erik. I didn't do anything for myself.

I wore the same old clothes as always. But Erik came back with a brighter smile.

We had food.

We had rent.

I did night jobs on the weekends and I brought in more money sometimes when I did bachelor parties.

Those were intense and wild, but I wasn't really...there...when men had sex with me.

I didn't know what happened, I just went to a place in my head when they did. They had sex with me.

I didn't have sex with them.

I used lubricant and sometimes I felt something. I just made the appropriate noises and I watched porn to be the best I could be.

Because when I went home and showered and Erik hugged me when he saw the fridge full and his new clothes?

His new clean clothes?

It was the world.

Even he noticed the good things piling up in the house. I was stocking us up so we wouldn't ever need to worry. I had enough money saved for rent over time.

I just had to keep being this girl.

I didn't know her name, I didn't recognize her, and I felt like the real Vivianne Valentine died the day Mamie died and I...fucked her over.

Sometimes I stared at the painting Mamie put on the wall and wondered if it was irony to watch and believe in love a long time ago—only to realize love didn't exist.

It was an illusion.

Not for people like me.

~

AND THEN NATURALLY I PLAYED THAT GAME FOR A FEW MONTHS. Sometimes when I was with men, I just zoned the fuck out.

I learned little tricks.

Using lubricant and having my own condoms. If not, I got on birth control, got tested after every single "client" and worked my ass off.

Sometimes I went on a few dates during the night.

One night I went on a date with a man who wasn't very nice at the dinner table nit picking what I ate.

That should have been my first red flag but Heather wasn't joking when she said sometimes the mean guys paid the most.

And I thought I would get paid.

I mean—I did.

The second red flag was when he wanted to check my pockets for any devices or anything like that. And when he didn't find any he seemed assuaged.

I didn't get it.

Not until we got to the hotel room.

And I felt the ominous feeling crawling up to my stomach, but by then it was too late.

The split lip was the least of it.

I stood in my bathroom in Mamie's apartment, having run out of the room when he was in the restroom, pressing ice against my face and trying not to look at the rest of the bruises blooming across my skin.

Erik was sleeping so I couldn't make noise.

I told myself I was fine.

I told myself it wasn't a big deal even if I couldn't sit.

I told myself I would be okay.

I laid there on the couch for a long time in the dark staring at the painting.

The Storm.

The metaphor for my life.

A storm.

I laid there feeling my vision blurring with how numbed out I felt. I looked down at my phone and realized in that moment—I turned eighteen tonight.

I stared at the Storm.

The moonlight beams hitting it at odd angles, making the light fracture out of the painting and I slowly sat up. Slowly.

"Is the painting moving..." I said to no one in particular. The shame clouding my thoughts. I slowly stood wincing as I did as I walked up to the painting in the dark.

"Mamie...what did you..."

I slowly put my fingertips to the halfway point since it took up most of the wall.

With careful consideration I took it off and shined my phone lights on it.

I always thought this was something passed down through

generations or a knock off. Erik had a comic book one in his room. This exact size and enormous.

So I don't know why I was unpacking the painting, slowly taking it out and thinking it might be worth something.

One side curled towards me as I took it out and I paused.

"What the…"

Lines. A compass.

"It's a…map?"

What the fuck?

I needed to go ask Greenie, but once I healed.

For tonight, I put the painting back and told myself I'd check on it later my heart racing as I looked up the history of the painting on my phone.

Once I had the information I needed, I waited a few days, went to Greenie.

"I can't do these gigs anymore," I told him. "I want something else."

He looked at me the same way he always had. Like he was assessing me.

"I found something in Mamie's room. A painting. It's one half of two." I explained to him a couple of nights ago that I looked up at the painting that Mamie had was one of two paintings. One of two.

The second half was lost in time.

The first half was mine.

"…when you put them together—"

Greenie shook his head in disbelief. "Treasure ain't real, raven."

Even though I had red hair now.

"But what if it is?" I asked him. "It's all I have now. Don't you know anyone else. Someone who can introduce me to someone else? I can work with them. I can figure this out—"

"raven—"

"Greenie!"

We both stopped and he sat back for a few seconds. I didn't know if he was going to say anything or let it simmer.

Finally, he breathed out another puff of his joint.

"All right, I'll see who I can call."

"And you'll help me find the second half of the painting?"

21

He waved a hand at me like letting me know he would and I walked away feeling something for the first time that I hadn't felt in the last year since Mamie died.

And I did too.

Hope.

I felt hope.

PRESENT DAY

4

KIERAN

PRESENT DAY

"Happy Birthday Luna!"

Luna, my god-daughter, hid her face into Lara's neck as everyone grinned. Dark curls to her elbows and little purple tulle dress combined made her look like a little doll.

But it was her eyes that gave her away.

Her father's eyes blinked all shy and adorably on her. I knew exactly who Luna's father was. And I knew for a fucking fact, he had no clue she existed.

My entire family intended to keep it that way.

Lara Ford, her mother and my...

Roommate.

Nothing romantic there.

Not for Lara anyway. Not when I knew she was still in love and always would be with Luna's biological father—Liam Sullivan.

Resident shit stick and all around douche bag after the shit he pulled with Lara from what little Killian told me. I pieced it together.

Lara stood holding her with a beaming smile.

"Mi amor, look—" she motioned to our family. The girls were losing it all around me. All the little girls my brothers had

I was celebrating Luna's birthday today. Out of all things.

A lot had changed for my family in the last five years.

24

Killian, my second oldest brother had met his wife Nisha.

They'd gotten married and had two little girls, Kiara who turned three a few weeks ago, and Marissa who was just turning one and learning to feed herself into a gnocchi coma.

Then, my oldest brother Aidan, met Sonya, and the two of them settled down.

Their twin girls were both two. Selin and Kiraz were the center of Aidan's world alongside Sonya.

Lara had moved in with me years ago after her baby daddy fucked up with her.

So Luna became my goddaughter. The absolute fucking apple of my eye. And right now?

Luna was shyly tucking herself into Aidan's body as he grinned down at her.

Never in my fucking life would I have imagined, Aidan O'Hara, the devil himself and former head of the O'Hara crime syndicate as a father. Let alone a father to two of his 'princesses.'

But there he was. Grinning as he fed Luna and grinning wider when she reached for her Mama.

Aidan was thirty-five now. But he had been the same guy who had taken over from our father Cormac after he'd been murdered.

I knew the story. He'd built the family legacy and empire and then he fell in love with Sonya.

My father had always made sure that I never wanted anything without feeling ashamed of myself, of wanting, and of needing anything that I could've ever asked for.

I was Aidan's placeholder.

Not really fitting in.

Not quite getting the grasp of things the way my older brother's did.

I never fit in with Aidan. Too big. Too tough. And entirely unlike me. He was the oldest, the one with the most pressure, and the most likely to not fail in the family.

I held onto Aidan's advice before he dipped out to go to Sonya.

I would *always* remember when Aidan fell for Sonya—because that was how I ended up on his throne.

Of blood and shadows.

Head of the family. Whatever that meant.

I sat back with Marissa crawling around my legs. I picked her up easily settling her into my lap.

"Are you running away?" I teased.

She tossed me a gummy smile and her stuffed whale toy, Wally that the girls lost their minds over.

"I'm good, sweets," I held her watching everyone fuss over cake and Killian sneaking in kissing Nisha while holding Kiara.

I watched everyone and realized my family was now enormous and everyone had someone.

Turns out, the O'Hara's could only have girls and the irony never escaped me.

In my arms Marissa mouthed something.

"Are you learning your words?" I adjusted her bow. "What are you trying to say?"

"Jooseeee."

"Juice?"

"Jooose."

"I can get you juice, sweets." I stood with Marissa and headed into the kitchen to fill her a little sippy cup of Joose.

She watched completely fascinated and staring at me in awe and excitement repeating Joose over and over again until Killian came up behind me and helped out laying out a few more cups.

"You're gonna need it."

His mismatched eyes—one aqua and one amber—watched Marissa in my arms smiling at him. "Hi, mini-luv. Did you steal Unca ?"

"Daddy," she reached for him and my brother's inky hair fell over his eyes as he took her into his arms.

He was my height but leaner in general as he held her helping me.

"Why are you pouring that much Joooose?" I pointed at the nine sippy cups or so he poured into.

"Because your niece summoned the other cats—" he didn't even finish as I heard a chorus of "juice" behind me and I turned to find the stampede of little feet. Tiny tulle dresses, tinier tiaras and happy smiles wandering over to us.

Killian's smile was wide as he watched them.

I bit back my laugh. "Ladies, ladies, there's plenty of Joose."

Sonya appeared in the doorway, laughing at the chaos. "Let me help."

Together, we managed the parade of princesses, passing out sippy cups and wiping sticky hands as we did.

And I spent the afternoon catering to whatever the tiny kids wanted of me aware that in another life maybe if I hadn't fucked up so bad—this could've been my life.

But not every one deserves a happy ending.

Especially not me.

5

KIERAN

Titan Midtown was quiet at this time.

It was early in the morning and Lara and Luna were visiting Teaser's, and I had to go see Reed Whittaker. CEO of Titan Security.

Sort of. I could've sworn Reed ran ops, his best friend, and my mentor. But he was settling down and having kids so I didn't think he wanted to talk to anyone.

Now? Reed was here hanging out and waiting for me.

Or so I thought as I walked down the familiar navy and silver trimmed halls his door was open and I heard a rattle from inside.

"Wooo!"

"Yeah, buddy, I know. That's Mama."

"Daddy...*Mama*..."

"She's pretty, isn't she?"

Sitting at his desk as I knocked was definitely Reed Whittaker, at thirty-four, he still somehow looked younger than his age.

Dark chocolate colored hair, storm-cloud eyes, and his signature white-shirt stretched across his chest. But it was the baby that stopped me.

"Please tell me that's your son."

He grinned as both of us looked down at an adorably chubby little kid on his lap blinking up at me with hazel eyes. He was the

28

spitting image of Reed save for those eyes. Those were all his moms.

"Say hello to Uncle, Rhys."

"Hullo," the baby on his lap waved a stuffed giraffe at me. "Daddy..." he looked like he was struggling to say something as I walked up. "Man."

"I didn't realize you had a kid."

"I'm quiet about him," Reed murmured with a softness I had never heard in his voice. "Otherwise, the horde of Alisha's fans will appear to kidnap him."

"I heard about that," I sat down in the chair to find Rhys's eyes on me. I waved at him.

Reed had gotten married to his model and social media content creator of a wife—Alisha.

It had been a fucking hilarious nightmare to find a dozen men protesting in front of Titan Midtown.

For her *not* to get married.

Reed had called the cops and they'd been handled, but it was fucking downright hilarious to everyone else.

Reed smiled down at Rhys. "He just turned two, Lish is out with Avani and Thierry took Theo out for a playdate, we're meeting up after this."

"Thierry?" DuPont. A former assassin was married to Reed's sister-in-law. I heard about that too. And their kid.

Reed nodded. "I have Rhys for the day, isn't that right, buddy? We're at work with Daddy."

"Work. Work!" Rhys was involved. And I saw on Reed's desk where there usually was a gun and knives or tech gadgets, there was a little bottle of milk, some baby snacks, and a toy pen and writing pad for kids.

"Do you wanna take notes while Daddy talks to his friend?"

"Yes." Rhys held up his toy phone as Reed laughed.

"No, we don't have any calls. But we can take notes for Uncle ." He handed his son his toy pen the size of a carrot. I bit back my laughter and failed even as I grew aware of Reed becoming a totally different person.

He had moved on.

I knew Reed for tearing into recruits. Not this version of him.

"Lish got him a little phone so he doesn't feel left out when I take calls," Reed smiled at me easier than he ever had. "Rhys likes to participate in everything. Everything she does, everything I do. He wants to be *involved*. Don't be surprised if he asks questions."

I laughed unable to stop myself with how serious the kid looked at me. He motioned his carrot pen.

"Mama."

"Yeah, buddy. That's from Mama. Tell me about Chicago, I got him occupied."

I filled in Reed about a few things, as Rhys pretended to write and take notes, giving up halfway through and pawing through his snacks. Reed grinned every so often passing him things. The two of them interacted with Reed knowing the kids needs.

He reminded me of Aidan.

"...I haven't hired anyone in forever after the merger with Talon," Reed explained. "But if you need bodies, you can take some of the Talon guys over. I know there's a dozen of them bored out of their minds. Should be fun for Leo."

Leo Romero was the equivalent of Reed over Chicago.

"I'll think about it," I told him. "Right now, I'm solid. Are you two going somewhere?"

"Yeah," Reed said. "I'm gonna give him a break from working and take him to his favorite bagel shop. Isn't that right, Rhys? You want a bagel today?"

"Beeegel."

I grinned. "With some Jooose?"

"Joose."

"I'm convinced all kids are trained in this," I quipped as Reed laughed with apparent joy.

"He loves coming out here."

I realized I'd never seen Reed so happy. Or this much emotion from him, but fatherhood...that shit changed people. It certainly changed Killian who juggled princess tiara's and pink tulle all over his house.

It should've warmed my heart, but I just blinked back my own emotions.

I had no right to be jealous.

I had no right to want what he had.

I had no right.

I fucked it up for myself.

But sometimes, I imagined Lara was my wife, Luna was my daughter—and I was someone's somebody.

Not fucking O'Hara.

I could've done that.

But I had been young and dumb.

I chose not to.

I finished my meeting with Reed to Rhys almost falling asleep in his arms. The sleepier the kid got the more Reed snuggled him like a little teddy bear in his winter suit.

"I don't want him getting sick, I don't like when he's uncomfortable," Reed murmured as he pinned Rhys to his chest in the baby carrier and then zipped his own jacket over him.

I made my way out to the streets where I could just pretend I was like everyone else. Not a man with a shadow in Devlin Rafferty, his dark hair held back with a beanie.

"Hey, boss. Ready?"

I was. My phone pinged as I got into my car.

I just bumped into Liam.

And he knows about Luna.

Because Liam fucking Sullivan didn't know shit about his daughter.

Well. *Fuck*.

My morning went south and fast.

6

VIVIANNE

"I THINK I KNOW WHO HAS THE SECOND PAINTING."

"Who?"

"Teo fucking DuPont."

"Businessman?"

"Mafia."

That was Greenie's update.

Over the last four years?

I had been running bigger and bigger cons, forging checks, doing everything but sleeping with men.

Not after that incident.

I never told anyone, but I didn't ever want to talk about how much money I lifted off fuckers. I did have Greenie find out who the guy was and I smashed up the guys car. We had a few guys rob him over the course of a year. That was fun.

My first year I went to different cities across the state and I pretended to be a lost tourist.

I dyed my hair flaming red and pretended to have accents while I worked with someone else lifting their wallets.

Something happened in my chest the more I worked in the shadier elements of life.

The less I gave a shit.

The less I wanted to. The former me was gone, buried somewhere so deep she didn't want to come back out. This me?

This me was putting Erik through college.

He was comfortable.

And I made sure he had no clue what his sister had to do.

The jobs got bigger for me and a lot smoother with me switching out my proverbial mask every single time I had to.

A ditzy college aged student. Through my gigs—I learned men were monsters.

They wore masks too. Just uglier than mine. I learned to use my body which had filled in and my looks for me.

Even at five-two I started taking self defense and I started becoming more fluid moving around as a whole.

Nobody knew me.

Sometimes, I pushed my younger self down and away to the same place where the seventeen year old girl in me died.

Erik had meals. Scholarship money. Clothes. Funds to pay for whatever he wanted including a bank account I dropped cash into every so often. Erik had it nicer.

He was going to Kingston Prep in New York full time and he often did summer classes to speed through.

At the rate he was going at nineteen?

He was set to graduate at twenty.

Erik didn't stop.

So I didn't stop working hard either.

The painting consumed me when Greenie filled me in about Matteo DuPont.

"He's mob?" I muttered one day in a basement room of Greenie's old apartment.

Erik might've lived in the city, but I moved around too much.

Most of the time I crashed in Mamie's apartment where the storm hung. I never moved out.

I couldn't.

I hated where I was, but every fancy apartment I viewed to move felt wrong. It felt off.

"He's head of the Irish syndicate, nobody fucks with him after he killed his father…" Greenie filled me on the rumors about Aidan O'Hara being a monster.

Even now, after years of this lifestyle, my stomach churned.

"How do I get through to him?"

Greenie looked at me like I was insane. "Get through? Raven—you ain't getting shit."

"Why the fuck not?"

Teo DuPont?" Greenie now looked paler. "Nobody fucks with him. Nobody. Rumor was a few years ago, he cleaned up some of the Bratva in town because they was fucking with him. You wanna be next?"

Teo? DuPont? The CEO of Roadster's was mafia?

I blew out a breath. "Greenie, I'm not giving up. I don't care who he is—"

"Raven, he will fucking make an example out of you—"

"Not if I don't get caught."

"You're insane," Greenie leaned back in his couch shaking his head at me. "You do a few insane jobs and it eats at your head—"

"Shut the fuck up," I stood up to my full height ready to tear into him. The years had changed me. Completely. "That's *my* fucking world on the line. You wouldn't get it. I need me an in to Aidan fucking O'Hara—and if it ain't you—I'm gonna fucking do it myself."

I grabbed my jacket off his couch and dipped out.

I didn't need Greenie anymore. I had resources. Folks to help me.

People who owed me money now. It felt fucking good to be here.

"Wait!" Greenie rushed after me. "Hang on! Just tryna take care of ya, Raven."

I stopped breathing out again in a sigh.

"Raven," Greenie turned me around a glint in his eyes different from before. Over the years I wondered if the drugs were making Greenie crazy because I couldn't explain why he was the way he was. "I'm looking out for ya. That's it. It's not that I don't want to help you—"

"So then help me—"

"I can't—"

"Why not!"

"Because O'Hara is ruthless!" Greenie snapped. "He will fucking kill you. And then he will find Erik and kill him too."

That made me pause. That tiny bit.

Erik was my entire world.

Greenie and I had done research on the painting. Before Mamie's family had it?

It had been stolen from the house of the Kennedy family in New York. But as far as I was aware?

They didn't have the second half. It was missing.

It was owned by them.

And nobody knew what the back of the map was. Rumor had it, it was treasure, but nobody knew what kind. So I went and dug further.

I found some folks in New York who were able to tell me a few years back what the potential was.

The former lover of a pirate king who married into the Kennedy family buried his treasure.

And she added the map he had to the back of the paintings.

The lovers were them through the seasons. Spring. Storm.

I had the second half. The first half was out there in the world somewhere.

When combined—it would open to money.

Enough money to fund a small country. And all fucking mine.

Some for Greenie for his help all through the years.

But mostly mine and Erik's.

I didn't know how Mamie got Storm. But I had it in my possession and Greenie had left it alone.

We took photos of our map and the rumor was the Kennedy family still had their half but nobody knew where.

I didn't know. I had spent the last few years searching desperately for it.

I didn't want a mafia don to stop me.

"What do I gotta do to get it?" I looked at him. "Anything. I can change my name, I can be whoever I want to be—"

"It doesn't work like that—" Greenie's brown-eyes were wilder now. "Don't you get it—"

"No!" I shouted back. *"I don't fucking get it! I don't get it because this shit has been my entire fucking life for so fucking long!"*

Nothing was going to take it from me.

Even if the thought of bringing my brother into this twisted me up? My brother had no fucking clue who I was.

He didn't know that his big sister was betting everything on a fucking map hidden behind a century old painting that would lead to something bigger.

He didn't know what I had done. Not the extent of it.

It was my everything. I held onto it like a mental health patient in a psych ward. Losing my shit with every single fucking breath.

I fell asleep some nights imagining what my life would be like never having to do this again. That painting was my salvation and my fucking obsession.

"This is my final job, Greenie. This is it. If anything happens to me, it all goes to Erik. I don't give a shit anymore."

I was prepared to die for Erik.

Would he miss me? Sure.

I would rather die than let Erik go through anything that I had. At the minimum the painting would pay for everything he wanted to be and then some.

"That painting is my everything, Greenie," I looked into his eyes. "Get me a way to get close to Aidan O'Hara."

He blew out a breath considering it for a long time before he finally said. "Word on the street is, he's got a girlfriend. Lives with him in there. They got a kid together."

That was a start.

"I need info. All of it."

I promise. One day I'm gonna give me and Erik and Mamie everything.

I promise.

7

KIERAN

"Boccoli."

"Clover."

Luna was coloring in the family seal that all of my brother's had gotten in honor of what had happened to us. It had been some of our first tattoos.

"Boccoli."

"Clover," I corrected gently. Luna shook her curls at me. "You have your father's eyes kid. It's a little weird."

"Boccoli."

"Fine. Broccoli it is."

She stuck her tongue out like the word was offensive.

In size and stature, she took after her mother, but in personality? She was completely her dad. A little mischievous. Sneaking off and doing things she shouldn't. Or coloring my arm tattoos.

Her dark curls were all over the place and her bow forgotten on the ground as Lara walked in.

"Carina! Mami has food!"

"Mami!"

I passed Luna off to her as Lara sat down with her daughter and lunch.

Everyone had someone but me.

And all I did want was someone. I wanted someone to hug me all the time. Like Lara had.

Someone who ran to me with happiness because I was her happiness. Someone who stayed.

I went to Liam's new home down the street.

An upscale townhouse in white and gold it was the most un-Liam like place ever.

I had a meeting with Leo Romero in an hour or so but first I had to talk to Lara and Liam.

"Liam is staying one block away from us."

I was trying to maintain my composure and keep my irritation in check. Not at Lara, but it was impossible to even be the slightest bit angry with Luna on my lap.

My daughter was coloring in my tattoos with giant markers and humming.

I sat perfectly still watching Lara eating lunch. I was trying to distract myself with my e-reader but I couldn't.

I couldn't focus.

And I didn't know how to even start to focus when I felt Luna coloring in and adjusting again and again.

She was my little girl even if she wasn't.

And I couldn't contemplate murder with her purple soft dresses.

On his other side was my companion, a massive orange presence that felt like more of an oversized pillow and not a cat.

Cheddar was the rescue had I had been given years ago.

And he was *obese*.

I was the only O'Hara that I knew not allergic to Cheddar, and Luna had fallen in love with him.

Now, the giant fur ball migrated between the space heater he loved and the kitchen where Luna knew how to sneak him tuna.

"Did she give him a treat again?" Lara asked biting back laughter.

I loved Lara like a sister at best.

At five-one max, she was a petite Latina with a formerly fiery temper, but not anymore.

Not since she left New York with her baby and started life over in Chicago with me. Lara and I became friends over the last few years but I felt next to nothing for her.

I thought maybe an arrangement of any sort would've helped me cope with the fact that my brothers weren't alone. And I was.

"Unca ."

I looked down at Luna where she was coloring, and where she was focused on the new tattoo he'd gotten on his sleeve. Her tiny fingers moved over his chest now.

"Unca...look."

"I see that, sweet pea. You're doing such a good job," I murmured at her artwork. "That's a nice color you picked. Green."

"Green. Broccoli."

"Close. Clover. Can you say clover?"

"Clova...Broccoli."

I wasn't proud of my tattoos at all. The shamrock I had was a momento of a past life I didn't want to remember.

Lara had one singular tattoo and it was a reminder enough to never be a dad and end up like my father.

All three of the O'Hara's had that brand tattooed on them.

As a reminder of all the crimes my father had committed and all the things I didn't want to end up as.

Lara never covered it up. So I didn't want to either.

But I always felt guilty for being a former prostitute, a former con-man and current mobster, and sometimes I wondered if Luna would be better with me. If she could pretend Killian or Aidan was her father.

And those thoughts made me feel ashamed of myself even more.

I didn't know what to do about my emotions.

I just knew they existed with me every single day.

"Are you okay?" 's eyes were on me worried. "You don't look okay."

I blinked back my emotions and nodded. "Fine."

"I know when you're lying to me."

Luna looked up at him again and pointed at his clover.

"Yes, sweet pea. Broccoli."

"Broccoli." She went back to coloring her broccoli in and I got a second to breathe and take in the colder air outside before Lara interrupted.

"Tell me why Titan wants to talk to you about a painting."

"Lucy Devereaux went and told Sonya a couple of years ago thankfully, that everything in Hyacinth Manor, the shelter Sonya runs, is worth millions. There's a painting in Hyacinth Manor. It's the second half of a set of two..."

I knew about the painting. I didn't give a shit why it was important or not.

I didn't care.

I just knew several international thieves wanted these two paintings.

And I happened to know where one was.

Sonya had a painting that was one half of two.

The second one had been lost in time.

Nobody knew who had it and nobody had found it ever.

The first one belonged rightfully to Sonya and she had put it somewhere safe.

"What is it?"

"The lore behind the painting is that it's a map. If you flip both of them over? It leads somewhere. Someone out there has the second half or the rumor is, the second half has turned up."

"You're serious. There's a treasure map inside a painting."

"Treasure." Luna piped in.

"Yes, sweet pea. Treasure and gold."

explained dryly that the Titans had heard a rumor the second painting had appeared. "Somewhere out in Hong Kong, and it's in Chicago right now. One of the Titans—Reina—traced it back to here. It's in the city."

"The second half," Lara mused.

I tipped my head back, eyes sharp. "And we made sure when Sonya dropped off the original painting, nobody knew where it was. Save for Sonya and the company she hid it inside, Nash Group. Specifically Natasha Nash. You don't know of her—"

"No."

"Nash Group has the painting. They are also tracking the second one and a bunch of operatives known as Talon, Kieran owns them are being sent to Chicago. Nash Group wants their hands on the second painting—"

"For the map?"

I shook my head. "They're collectors. They want the painting for the sake of having it. Natasha Nash likes a complete set. Talon works inside of Titan so they're just doing her bidding."

"And the person who has the second painting?"

"There's a jewel thief in town Lucy Devereaux is familiar with. Vivianne Valentine. Vivianne is a huge catch and so besides Titan Chicago, Talon, and Nash Group—" I broke off with a wild laugh. "The FBI is in town too."

I clapped my hands over my mouth as I set my sandwich down.

"You're telling me four different organizations are in town, lookin for Vivianne ?"

"And Vivianne herself has to be in disguise. Honestly, sometimes I wish Sullivan wasn't such a dipshi—shoot. Sorry, sweet pea. Because I'd just ask him to use his version of Oracle, find Vivianne , get the second painting and be done with it. Technically Titan and Talon are all the same team. They work together. But the Fed's want Vivianne and they've wanted her for a long time."

"I didn't even know Lucy Devereaux was a jewel thief until right now—"

"Former jewel thief. She reformed once she met Adam. But Lucy says Vivianne 's trouble. Younger. Bolder. Maybe twenty-one. Maybe. Lucy thinks she's hunting for the second painting."

"But Sonya has the second—" I broke off at Lara's knowing gaze. "Vivianne thinks the second painting is in Chicago."

"Because Sonya was staying here." I pointed to the manor. "Three years ago. Vivianne doesn't know about Sonya and Aidan. Not many people do. Aidan never goes out with her in society and so Vivianne thinks—"

"*Dios,*" she whispered. "Vivianne thinks *you* have the painting."

"She's in for a rude surprise when she realizes it isn't here. She can try and break in all she wants. Which is why I have Josh and Nadine coming over today."

"But if she breaks in—Vivianne might hurt you."

"No," I smirked feeling a dark and devious. "She wants the map.

41

I'm going to give her a fake and Titan Chicago wants to catch her before the Feds do."

"You think Vivianne Valentine is going to break into your bedroom?"

"I know she is. And when she does, I'll be ready."

"So...what do we do about your problem since you know mine?"

Since her problem was six-feet-four inches of green-eyed computer hacker who lived five buildings down.

And I didn't really feel anything for the guy since the Cold War between him and Kieran was one we didn't really speak of anymore.

I knew Aidan was good with him because of Sonya, but that's about all I was invested in.

"I'll go talk to him."

"I'll take care of Luna."

"Broccoli!" Luna chirped.

"Clover, sweet pea. Try clover."

"Broccoli."

LUNA'S BOW WAS ALREADY ASKEW.

I adjusted it on her head as she slept on my chest curled up like the day she came home from the hospital.

Dark curls everywhere and I smiled down at her chubby little cheeks smushed into me.

I didn't even hold her for a few weeks because she'd been so tiny, she looked unreal.

Now, she was much bigger but the same as the orange fur ball sleeping next to me.

My brain was doing numbers and figures while she slept.

The strings of pubs I wanted to put up, high end coffee shops Sonya had suggested, Nisha's restaurant pop-ups we wanted to introduce to Chicago.

I had to go down with Devlin Hart when a few bodies had shown up at the port shipping containers and I knew it was nasty

42

for our name to be anywhere near it. That was going through the cops.

I'd been busy, texting one-handed, holding Luna with the other as she snuffled. I adjusted her little blanket.

Cheddar and Luna were a fucking team.

A team.

And her mother, Lara was currently over visiting Liam.

Liam Sullivan.

The man who had moved from New York to Chicago to fucking come see his daughter and his girl.

I knew about Liam. I knew five years ago he fucked up on an assignment and lost Lara.

I knew all about him and his mistakes costing her to the point where she'd been pregnant and scared with me.

I knew he was somehow related to Gabriel's wife.

Liam had pissed off a lot of people.

And Lara and Liam had broken up years ago. Before he knew about Luna.

Now, he was back. No doubt fucking determined to get Lara back in his life.

Now that Luna was…his girl.

I didn't know all the fucked up things Liam had done.

But I knew it wasn't that much of a jump from what I had been. I knew. I talked to Sonya all the time. I knew what she felt about me.

I had been a former drug addict and alcoholic crushing on Reed's sister-in-law Avani. Hard. And I'd missed her.

Now Avani was married. She was happier than ever from what little I knew. Just a little.

And I was still…me.

Luna's godfather—sure. But me.

I was . Just .

The man Luna leaned on for everything and the one person in the world Lara trusted. But not loved. Not enough.

Maybe that part of me, the boy I had been felt for Liam who had sobered up and realized how badly he messed up.

Chasing down Lara cities just to apologize to her.

43

I heard the click of the front door late enough for me to know, Lara was back. I slowly got up adjusting Luna so she was laying with Cheddar.

"The two of them are out. You good?"

She shook her head motioning me to follow her out of the living room. Far enough to have privacy, close enough away from Luna to keep an eye on her.

Lara quickly whisper-hissed and explained it to me.

"He kissed Isobel?" I fought to keep my voice down. *"That son of a—"*

"And then he says he said my name when kissing her."

I broke off, looking down at her. "Huh?"

Something about this wasn't adding up. I listened as she explained further, feeling my frown deepen with understanding.

"When he kissed Isobel, he said your name?"

"Yes."

"And he stopped kissing her and told her about you?"

"Yes."

"That doesn't sound very scummy."

"What?"

"Think bout it," I said, watching her face carefully as I did the math. "He's in love with this girl for twenty-nine years. He meets you. He sees you and dates you and treats you right—Isobel comes back and sure, he kisses her but that's like a 'I'm so happy you're alive kiss' not a 'Let me cheat on my girlfriend kiss' you know?"

"What? Kissing is kissing, ."

"No, it isn't. I made out with Gianna all the time. My dick felt nothing for her. I just did it because it was empty for me and a replacement for something else. I'm a guy, Lara. I have issues. I can kiss one girl and think about another."

"That's disgusting."

"Yeah, but at least I know it. Liam sounds like he didn't. He might've been relieved to see Isobel but his only thought was about you. You've never kissed one man and thought about anyone else?"

"But he kissed her while he was with me."

"True." I tipped my head back, feeling the weight of my own

44

experiences. "Pretty shitty of him. But Liam's always been...somewhere in the middle of good and evil."

Just like me.

"Between cheater and faithful man. In the past at least. Between Titan and Talon. Between his family and the world. Sounds like he's been caught in the middle every single time. Shit sucks." I rubbed the back of my neck, remembering my own middle grounds. "I would know."

"You think there's a difference in how he kissed Isobel versus me?"

Something dark and reckless stirred in me. "Stay still, Lara."

My voice dropped as I moved closer, dipping my head before she could react.

I pressed my mouth to hers. Quick, intense, but impersonal.

A kiss of relief, of survival, of *thank-god-you're-alive.*

"That is how I kissed you in relief to know you're okay."

I moved in again. "That is how I kiss my girlfriend," I murmured, showing her the difference. This one was familiar, comfortable, but without real heat.

I held her face in my hands for the third kiss, letting myself show her what real want felt like.

What it meant to kiss someone you actually desired.

My hands remembered every curve as I lifted her, tongue claiming her mouth with an intensity that surprised even me.

When I set her down, we were both breathing hard. "Feel the difference?"

Her hands gripped my shoulders as I growled into the kiss, showing her exactly what desire felt like. What it meant to want someone completely.

I pulled back with a gasp, trying to steady myself. "That is how I kiss the woman I want to fuck. Feel the difference?"

She nodded, looking dazed.

"There's a difference," I managed, setting her down carefully. "Between you and someone else. Between you and Isobel. Between what Liam wants and what he says he doesn't."

I forced a smirk, pushing down whatever this feeling was. Just a

45

connection I needed. A body. Lara had never been my girl. Nor would she ever be.

I was in my own purgatory of my own making now.

And I couldn't even complain about it.

"Give him a chance, Lara. He did fuck up. But he's also an idiot like me. A lonely idiot. He moved to be around you." I saw the hesitation in her face. "You don't have to introduce Luna to him. But maybe just see if his word holds up? Who's it gonna hurt?"

Lara was quiet.

And I couldn't resist feeling a little bit of my old self coming back.

"Wanna make out again?"

8

VIVIANNE

Thanks for the new clothes.

And groceries?

Got 'em too!

Everyones jealous. I have the best family.

Ha. Ha. Broke med students can't buy lunch?

Broke med students can't buy beans, sis.

Thanks for everything I got it. I'm good. Ollie and I are going out tonight for drinks.

Roomie and I are going out tonight to celebrate his team beating the Dark Knights. Rival hockey team for Astor U.

Look at you making friends.

Oooooooo hockey

LOl sis. Roomie's got a girlfriend. She might be coming too.

What are you doing tonight?

I LOOKED DOWN AT THE BLUEPRINTS OF THE O'HARA FAMILY mansion Greenie had somehow gotten his fucking hands on.

Greenie worked as a janitor at a real estate office every other day of the week.

Mercury Group had the blueprints to a lot of buildings. Part of why Greenie worked there.

Over the years their security was solid, but they always overlooked cleaning staff.

I had gone there before breaking and entering but I got caught twice by Titan Security. And I almost caught the boss-man himself Lucas Devereaux with his wife.

Greenie had nabbed the O'Hara mansion blueprints giving me a chance to go over it.

The woman who was living with Aidan O'Hara, Greenie didn't know her name. Apparently Aidan was a private man.

But I'd find out at some point. The second half was in his house. Inside the manor. I just had to figure out where.

> Hanging out with a friend. Nothing much. Enjoy your night. Be safe.

> Don't do anything stupid.

> You know I won't. See ya.

I was sitting in my living room. My heart heavier than it had ever been realizing, I was probably going to die. I wasn't going to get the treasure.

But I made Greenie promise to tell Erik. Take care of him. Until he finished school. I had enough in the bank to drop into Eric's name.

On paper?

Mamie never died. All those payments dropped into my account, then went to Erik. Little people were never noticed by the government.

This heist was my last one. Erik would be fine.

He will be fine.

I wiped my eyes at the thought of not making it to twenty-five. But I'd be fine.

I stared at the Storm, aware that there was a new storm coming my way.

I needed to do surveillance on O'Hara's home. I needed information. And a way in. Anything at all.

O'Hara barely had cleaning staff that they vetted and checked. Plus, with a baby? He'd be extra careful.

But I didn't give up easily.

Making a list of potential routes I could go, I began doing my homework. I couldn't study security rotations from close up, but I could go to the building across from the O'Hara's.

When there? I couldn't find anything.

"They have a secret entrance and exit, the only people who leave are the wife and her daughter. Dark hair, dark eyes." I told Greenie this much.

"No blind spots in cameras?"

"None, they're discreet as fuck."

Greenie nodded. "That's because he's got every reason to be paranoid."

I saw the tiny woman holding her baby and walking to the park.

The car behind them shadowing them and I knew O'Hara had guards on her.

I tried to look into private chefs, nanny's, and other angles, but not only did the O'Hara's only use people they trusted?

I'd be vetted within an inch of my life.

Even if Greenie came up with a profile for me?

It was too risky.

I felt like every which way I turned, I was hitting a wall which meant, I needed a new angle. And I needed a way in. Especially with the mom. I focused on her.

If I could separate her from her kid, and Aidan? I could get through with her.

I didn't know why, but my gut told me so.

Mamie would be disgusted at my thinking but I knew better than.

I knew what I had to do.

I was going to break the fuck into the O'Hara manor if it was the last thing I did.

Because I was tired of being the girl who wrapped herself up in lies. Every dinner, every dollar burned in my throat. The old stories about love and the price of freedom in my memories now.

Love was carrying the truth so nobody else had to. It was always my job to protect for my family.

To sacrifice so Erik wouldn't have to.

I spent the next few weeks plotting.

THE GALLERY CIRCUIT I WAS IN WAS INTERESTING ENOUGH.

The Philippe Stern Gallery opening was exactly the kind of pretentious art world event I had learned to navigate—all air kisses, overpriced wine, and people who spoke in hushed tones about "the artist's bold exploration of post-modern angst.

Perfect hunting ground.

I'd spent two days preparing for tonight.

The black cocktail dress was borrowed from a client who owed her discretion, the shoes stolen from a department store with laughably bad security, and the vintage Cartier watch was a gift from a lonely banker who'd paid her to pretend to be his girlfriend at his ex-wife's wedding.

The invitation had cost her three hundred dollars and a favor to Tommy Ruiz, who specialized in high-quality forgeries of a different sort.

I turned to find James Whitmore approaching with a champagne flute in each hand and that predatory smile she remembered too well.

Investment banker, terrible in bed, but very well connected. More importantly, he was the kind of man who enjoyed showing off his "discoveries" to other wealthy collectors.

"James." She accepted the champagne, letting her fingers brush his longer than necessary. "I didn't expect to see you here."

"Expanding my horizons. Art is the new cryptocurrency, haven't you heard?" He moved closer, and she caught the expensive cologne that couldn't quite mask the desperation. "I've been thinking about you."

"Have you?" I tilted my head, letting interest flicker in my eyes. "I've been keeping busy."

"Still in the...consultation business?"

The question was loaded with innuendo, but Vivian had learned to weaponize men's assumptions about her.

Let them think what they wanted—it made them underestimate her, and underestimation was her greatest advantage.

"I've pivoted," I said, taking a sip of champagne. *Bleh.* "Art advisory now. Helping private collectors identify pieces with... potential."

It wasn't entirely a lie.

I was helping myself identify pieces with potential.

"Really? That's fascinating. I'm actually looking to diversify my portfolio."

"What kind of pieces interest you?"

"Something with history. *Provenance.* The kind of thing that tells a story."

Perfect.

"There's going to be a private sale next week. Very exclusive. Estate liquidation from a family that's been collecting for generations."

James perked up. "I heard rumors, but I thought it was invite-only."

"What kind of pieces?"

Now we're talking.

9

KIERAN

"Sup, Nadine."

It didn't matter what kind of girl was my type—I was pretty sure, Nadine Forrester, was everyone's type.

At five-six, she had all my attention without trying.

Ambiguously mixed, raven black hair pulled back into a high ponytail, deadly as a viper and sharp tongued in a way that would stop traffic in any country.

Nadine was graceful and deadly at the same time. Her dark eyes glittered as she watched me walking in.

"Sup, kid."

"I'm only twenty-six."

"And I'm older than you," she said dryly, her full lips quirking into that smile that told me maybe sometimes she knew how she wanted to kill me.

"Maybe I'm into that," I snorted as silently as a wraith Joshua Ivanov appeared. Her partner-in-crime.

Six-feet-six inches of pure menace and ice.

I could never tell if Nadine and Josh were together or if they were…with benefits.

I could see Nadine using him for what she needed.

And usually I had radar for that shit.

"Still not my type." She shot back leaning against Josh. Definitely using him.

And Josh didn't look like he cared.

"Aw, come on, Nadine—"

I got cut off when Josh stepped half in front of her frowning at me. Not because he didn't like me. He didn't like me liking Nadine.

"Lawless is in the back," he muttered, his face uncovered for once.

His jaw set tight as he watched me, his expression almost regal. Compared to Nadine's viper like beauty, Josh was ice.

Ivanov, was an anomaly. Odd. Pale brown-eyes.

Platinum hair. No doubt Russian or something or another. Over the years I learned he was protective over Nadine. Did I *know* Josh had a thing for her? No. Did I *know* flirting with her would rankle him inside and out? Maybe.

Did I still do it on purpose?

Hell yeah.

I grinned as his silvery-hair head dipped closer, watching Nadine turn to him in confusion. Nadine doesn't have a fucking clue.

Some things never changed—trained operatives could spot a threat across a crowded room but couldn't see potential love standing right next to them.

Unlike New York, the Chicago Titans operated differently.

They ran cooler, harder, always on edge with the city's constant power shifts.

Their tower stretched toward the sky like another K2, all glass and steel and secrets.

This wasn't just another office—it was a fortress designed by Reed with Mercury Group to be the best.

My fortress, in a way, since they worked with the O'Haras more often than not.

Reina Lawless sat somewhere down the hall, the click of her keyboard a steady rhythm.

"Hey, you're here. Did you upset Josh again?" Reina Lawless had chocolate hair pulled into a low braid at the back.

She was the tech specialist here overseeing everything and a younger member of Titan from what I knew.

Reina Lawless was bright and often the one feeding information to Leo Romero, her boss.

"He's always upset."

"He is not," she frowned. "He's just protective of everyone."

Yeah, I knew that much. It was a lot like riling up Killian.

I just pressed the right buttons occasionally by flirting with Nisha who laughed it off easily since we were friends and Killian appeared pissed off as usual.

"Where's Leo today? He's not coming?"

"Nah, he's gotta bury a body."

I made a face and Reina Lawless giggled.

"What's new?"

Reina's smile dipped and her green eyes turned down to her keyboard. "We might have a tiny situation."

"That's never good," I muttered.

"No, but this one is a bit weird." Reina Lawless turned her computer around. "Have you ever seen this?" It was an old classical painting. Of two people running through a storm.

"No, what the fuck is that?"

Had I seen it before?

Why did it look like a style of painting I had seen before?

Reina Lawless shifted in her seat. "You might have not seen this one, but have you seen this one?"

And then she showed me a second one of two people painted on a swing with flowers all around them.

I gaped when the recognition hit me. "Hang on, that's the painting in—"

"Sonya Amin's Haven?" Reina Lawless nodded. "This is the second half of that painting. It's two of them. One half is two lovers hanging out, and the other is them running through the fields home. It's called Spring. The second one is Storm. They're two halves of a whole but in 1912 one half was stolen and nobody knew where it went."

Reina Lawless explained that Nadine had people on the ground

54

who worked for Titan and they noticed a man was asking around about it.

About who owned it.

"And somehow they think I own it?"

She looked a little uneasy, her green eyes unable to look at me. "Aidan asked us for some things when you took over…"

"Which is…"

"He never wanted anyone to know it was you, not until you let it be known so on the streets, Nadine never put the word out of you being in charge and she let people think it was still Aidan."

Confused I shook my head. "Wait what—"

"So, when people come crawling to steal from you or do anything, our informants can take care of you—" she broke off quickly rambling and explaining my big brother had apparently never told a soul I was switching with him as the head of the family.

Which was fucking news to me. At my frown Reina Lawless continued to explain.

Criminals and intelligence alike thought I was Aidan.

"Are you fucking kidding me?"

"So that's how we know, she wants to steal from you—"

"She?"

"This man his name is Jonathan Greenfield. Otherwise known as Greenie. He's a small time dealer in a bad neighborhood. He asked around Downtown about your family and this painting. Somehow someone thought you might have it. Which Nadine attributed to Sonya."

This was a little convoluted.

"Hang on, someone thinks or found out, Sonya had the other half. Because Sonya lived with Aidan years ago, they think…"

"They think you and Lara are Sonya and Aidan. Greenie is tied to someone we know. Her name is Vivianne Valentine. She goes by the name of Aldridge but she popped up on Nadine's radar a few years ago for crimes in Chicago."

Reina Lawless pulled up Jonathan Greenfield's photo and I saw a tired looking man with brown-eyes.

And then she pulled up a photo of a raven-hair woman, way too young, too thin, and dark shadows under eyes.

But even despite that, her higher cheekbones, sharp bone structure made her look ethereally beautiful.

"This is Vivianne Valentine. Nadine suspects from the intelligence she got, that this woman is the one who wants to break into the O'Hara manor."

"For the painting we don't have?"

"It's bad intel. Greenie doesn't know. We do."

Reina Lawless explained that Greenie had been fed the same information as most criminals.

Usually, when people found out that it was Aiden they left everything alone because of shift, it invited vulnerability.

And Aidan wouldn't want that with Luna at home.

"Way to look out big bro," I muttered.

"But he did you a favor, people on the ground who know about you? Told Greenie about Aidan. Now this girl thinks she can break in and take it. We suspect it's her because we are ninety percent sure of this—"

"She has one half."

"And she's looking to fill the other."

I sat back. "This is ridiculous. How do you know this?"

Reina Lawless chewed her bottom lip. "I called Reed and talked to his sister-in-law. Lucy."

"Lucy Whittaker told you that?"

Reina Lawless nodded. "She said she was the one who told Sonya years ago to put the painting into a vault with Nash Group. Natasha Nash owns it now. And we're not strangers to Lucy's background."

Lucy was a former jewel thief.

Now, she was married to Reed's brother, and a mom-to-be. A reformed thief.

"Lucy says, she suspects Vivianne might have one half. She asked her contacts out in New York and she said the only reason someone is hunting for one is because they have the other. And right now Vivianne thinks you have one."

What the fuck did I even say?

"A potential break-in might happen? I'm guessing Nadine is tracking this with you?"

Reina Lawless dipped her head. "Nadine says her contacts are going to give Greenie misinformation leading Vivianne to your doorstep."

"Why?"

"Because Lucy Whittaker says both of the paintings put together form a map—"

"A treasure map?"

Was she fucking serious?

"And Lucy thinks if we find it? It could lead to something bigger. Reed wants to follow through with this, because he trusts Lucy. So now..." Reina Lawless sighed.

Her other counterparts Nikolai and Damien were out on jobs so it was just Reina.

"Everyone in New York. Titan and Nash Group is invested. They want to catch Vivianne Valentine. Because she might know more than we do about the painting."

And everyone wanted their hands on it now, because they realized—Vivianne just exposed her hand to having it.

Every major player now wanted her head.

"Why can't we just pick her off the street?"

"Because Leo wants to see how it plays out. He wants her to show her hand first. We've got eyes on her, she's going to New York to visit her nineteen year old brother, Erik. He's a sophomore at Kingston Prep. Scholarship student." She turned a little pink. "I might be going undercover to spy on him. See if he's connected in anyway."

I blinked. "You?"

She shrugged lightly. "Leo thinks it'll be fun, besides he's nineteen—"

"You're twenty-four."

"I know. But I've never left my office, it'll be fun." Reina Lawless sighed. "Besides, with everyone watching Vivianne she won't even know it's all a trap for her until we catch her. Come on , it'll be funnnn."

"Only you guys would think that."

"But you know it's true."

I did.

It would be fun.

"Undercover in college, huh? Did you even go?"

"No," she turned red. "But—"

"It'll be funnnn." I laughed. "All right. I'm in."

10

VIVIANNE

I KNOCKED ON ERIK'S DORM TO HEAR A MAD SCRAMBLE ON THE other side and a feminine moan cut off.

Yuck.

No way my brother's got a girl.

"Ollie," I heard a feminine whisper. Dorm room walls were thin. "Your jeans."

"It's all good, *cara.*"

Ah. My brother's roomie. And his girlfriend were messing around in there.

Hopefully not with my brother. I shuddered at the thought considering I thought sex was repulsive.

My brother was probably buried in his books somewhere.

A messed haired raven-hair with brown-eyes cracked the door open, and stuck his head out, and even from here I caught a glimpse of the hickies on his neck and his bare chest.

"Hi. Can I help you?"

"Is my brother in?"

"Shit," his eyes widened. "No, Erik's at the library."

"He told me he'd be here."

"He ran out because he forgot a book."

Right. "Thanks."

He gave me a grateful smile since I clearly interrupted him and his lady.

I walked out of the dorm hallway and to the library on campus. It was autumn, and the air was really crisp in the middle of the term, where kids with money all kind of ran around.

Gothic architecture, Ivy covered buildings, this was the kind of place my brother deserved to be at.

I fucking knew he loved it here, so I had to work even harder to make sure he didn't show up with his ripped clothing.

Erik was always at the library or at school. He spent most of his time learning and I knew he was on track to graduate in three years instead of four.

I came to see him to tell him not to kill himself.

The irony. I walked into the olden day looking library and I searched all around until I found Erik in the basement study areas. Half asleep on his textbook.

I sat down next to him and he didn't even notice. My brother's situational awareness was at zero.

Survival instincts nonexistent which only made my heart clench more as I adjusted my red hair under my ball cap and my takeout bag for him.

At six-one now, he looked comical folded in one himself. Kingston Prep hoodie on and ripped jeans artfully styled.

His golden hair falling over his eyes and I knew if I woke him up he'd have half of his textbook on his face.

"Yo." I nudged him. "You got ink on your face." My brother clumsily lurched awake and I laughed. "Easy, just me."

He blinked several times, those brown-eyes of his meeting mine lazily, and I blinked back my emotions underneath my mask at how hard he worked.

"Sis," he breathed and then I was folded into his hug. I laughed easily inhaling his cologne I got him for Christmas. "Good to see you."

"You too," I laughed lightly. "Got you lunch."

I'm gonna miss him.

"No way, what—"

"Chinese food, look it's not real Chinese food, it's New York

Chinese food, but it's just as good—" I broke off laughing as he began rifling through it.

I would murder someone for New York Chinese food. I didn't know when chicken wings and fried rice became a thing?

But whoever put it together? Deserved cold hard cash.

"Sis, we gotta go outside," he began packing up his things now alive. *Boys.*

Food always worked with him.

"I was actually thinking we could eat this somewhere else, if you have time?" I shrugged trying to stay calm.

"Yeah, yeah," he stood and I noticed he looked a little thinner than usual, which wasn't like him. "Where are you coming from? I didn't know you were in town."

I kept my voice down as I helped him pack up into his bag.

"Why is your stuff ripped?" I asked him motioning to his bag. "I send you money."

He looked embarrassed now on his face. All gangly limbs and boyish charm.

"Uhhh, I don't like always spending it," he shrugged gathering up his books. "It's cool. It's a look."

"It is not a look," I pointed at him. "I'm buying you a backpack today along with everything else."

"Everything else?" I began walking with the takeout not to attract anyone's attention as Erik followed me.

I needed one last thing to take care of him. I had already dropped a reasonable amount of money into his account.

"Where are we going?"

"You'll see."

∼

"WHAT THE HELL?"

Erik looked around the apartment.

Not too far from Kingston Prep, there was a set of apartments I found which were a bit more high end, but still affordable for the city.

I held up the keys as I walked into the furnished home. "This is all yours."

My brother gaped looking around. "*What?*"

I grinned at his expression. "It's all paid for. You own it now."

It had been one of the last jobs I'd done. It was a sweet deal for what he had now.

"Vivianne, this is insanity—"

"No, it's home." I handed him the keys. "You want some water, your fridge is stocked." And he had a housekeeper since college kids and all.

"This is…" he looked around. "This is all mine?"

"Mhm, it hasn't been bought in years. Some security guy lived here before you, so it's got all these neat safety features too..."

The landlord had praised Nathan Wyatt for improving building security whoever he was.

He'd owned this apartment years ago before selling it.

And I bought it up.

Erik dropped his ripped backpack on the ground looking around a little lost. I grinned setting out the food.

Watching his reactions to things would never not be funny.

"What's up?" I said biting into an egg roll. It was warmer now. Not as crunchy.

"Sis...this is insanity." He looked around in awe. "This is my apartment?"

Erik always had a way of trying to make himself smaller and minimize himself and right now he was wandering around like a lost puppy before coming to look at the island.

"This is the biggest space I've ever been in."

And I knew that.

I knew.

"It's all yours," I continued eating. This space was everything I could've ever dreamed of him living in.

Along with the dark wood floors that probably cost more than anything else he had ever experienced, there was the sleek marble island that I was sitting on. Stainless steel appliances.

He could pretend he was in a cooking show.

There was even an abstract sculptures in the corner.

It was all done up in style.

"How did you manage?" He didn't know what I did.

I shrugged. "It just kinda worked out."

Some stroke of luck.

The food tasted like nothing as I swallowed it.

I suppose in my mind I thought at this moment would be momentous for me, just being able to give him a real home, but I realize that the layers of ice that had frozen over the younger version of me, felt to nothing.

It just felt like yet another thing off of my checklist. These were all of the pieces to keep him protected for the rest of his life.

Without me.

"Vivianne ."

"I'm serious. Eat something," I motioned to the food. "It's good for you."

Erik slowly took the outstretched lo mein in my hand. "Vivianne ..."

"Take the apartment, Erik. It's already yours."

Erik took in the built in bookshelves with medical textbooks. Everything I have was already his.

Everything I ever did...was for him.

I blinked back my emotions knowing he was watching.

He didn't know this was the last time he'd see me.

I had no doubt Matteo DuPont would absolutely fucking kill me if I got caught.

And if I didn't?

Loss in this field was inevitable.

A storm was coming for me.

And I was terrified of it.

I smiled at Erik. "How's your dinner?"

"You're insane."

I laughed outright the sound echoing in the kitchen.

11

KIERAN

"I NEED YOUR HELP."

I didn't really want to go to Liam Sullivan for help. But the guy was a cybersecurity genius.

He invented a program that might be helpful for me with Titan tracking Vivianne, I wanted a leg up too.

After my meeting with Reina, I knew that Titan was tracking everything happening.

But they were still in organization and they had a lot going on. I didn't want to risk anything happening to my family because of institutional oversight.

I did trust Reina, but I also knew that she was going undercover at Kingston Prep. Which meant even if I relied on her?

I couldn't fully.

I needed another way in.

I wanted to know all about her. Vivianne Valentine.

Luna was sitting on Liam's chest, coloring in his tattoos on his collar. Every so often he threw a ball to Cheddar who ran and came back.

"With?" He said it casually as Luna adjusted again who was coloring with concentration.

I sat down and filled him in and he frowned the more I talked.

His features growing more and more alarmed. Slowly, Liam sat up and moved Luna to the side a little so he could watch me.

It was a little eerie.

Liam and Kieran were two guys that no matter what you did, they were a little intense to interact with.

"You have a jewel thief who wants to steal a half of a painting you don't have. Sonya has the other one?…the Nash sisters have the first original."

"Correct."

"The second one is with Teo…"

"Nadine thinks Vivianne has an imitation of the second one," I explained. "We think she has it and she's searching to complete her set."

"What do you need?" Liam asked.

"Your version of Oracle." The program Liam had. "It's the only one we know of to find anything extensively."

"You want me to find Vivianne ?"

"Yes."

"And you want her captured?"

"Yes."

"Are my girls in danger?"

Not likely. She wanted the painting not the girls.

"I don't know."

Liam looked down at Luna who wanted to color him in all the way. He was protective as fuck about her now more than ever.

"Do I have to take them to my home?"

"Probably. Eventually. I'll talk to Lara when I get more info from you."

"Which is? I'm taking them home with me tonight. I don't care about your info."

I figured he'd say that. "Vivianne is in Chicago. She hasn't made a move—"

Liam sat up then, his eyes sharpening with an eerie green light in them as he tucked Luna into his bare chest more protectively.

"Sorry, shortcake. Let me help you."

"Mistake," she pointed at the mark on his chest. "No."

Liam licked his thumb and wiped it away for her. "There you go, shortcake."

"Dank you."

Something in my chest tightened at how easily he handled her now. I found out from the moment Lara told me about them, that Luna had wandered off into the street and found him.

Bumped right into him at a busy intersection and held onto his cane he had.

Like she was meant for him.

As had Lara.

"You're good with her," I murmured.

"Focus, my girls are in danger because of some painting and thief you wanna catch—You couldn't ask Lucy Devereaux to contact her?"

"Not if I want Adam pissed, Lucy is out of commission."

"Since when?"

"Since she was pregnant with twins. She's like halfway along and ready to murder everyone."

He gaped. "Lucy and Adam got *married*?"

I tipped my head wearing a bored expression.

Five years ago? All these people were single.

Now? It was just me.

"Finally. He said he'd do it once he finished his residency so he had the time. You can find Vivianne . And we can get rid of this whole problem."

"And what are you gonna do with Vivianne when I find her?"

"I don't know. But that's on me and Titan Chicago. If you find her—"

"I'll help you find Vivianne but I want a part of this. I'm not about to let my family be in any kind of danger."

"Deal."

"Deal," Luna squealed giggling. "Deal."

12

KIERAN

"You sure she's coming here?" I asked, voice low but edged with something I couldn't quite mask.

Liam was pacing—those long legs covering the floor like he was trying to outrun the weight in his chest. When Liam looked uneasy, it meant only one thing: his daughter was in danger. And no matter what, Lara's safety was everything to him.

Something about this whole setup felt off. Even I could feel it—a gnawing tension I couldn't shake.

"What's the matter?" I tried to sound casual, adjusting my shirt but failing to hide my own rising unease. "You don't look so good."

"No," Liam admitted, shaking his head slowly. "I don't like this. Why would she come here? She's a thief—stubborn and reckless— and her intel is outdated. Why stick around Chicago this long?"

Nadine leaned forward, her dark braid swinging with purpose.

"I think she's got someone here in the city. But we can't find any solid connections. Vivianne seems to be alone."

"On paper," Liam muttered, eyes sharp as they scanned the data on the screen.

He checked his phone, and I caught the photo—a rare moment of peace. Lara and Luna, wide smiles, laughter frozen in time. Lara holding Luna close, grinning at the camera. And there it was— Liam's worry, etched deep in his eyes.

I wanted to tell him to go home. To stay safe. But this was his fight too.

"You think she has a partner?" I asked.

"No," Nadine shook her head firmly. "Vivianne doesn't do relationships. Just flings. She's too guarded."

"Oracle," Nadine commanded, voice sharp and precise. "Search for Vivianne Valentine."

The screen flickered, then flooded with data. "Subject alive. Current residence: Chicago."

"That's impossible," Nadine frowned. "I've checked every address. The only places we can trace are an old apartment and Greenie's place."

I watched Liam's eyes sharpen with focus. "When I traced Lucy through Adam, I could only find her because I knew him. His patterns, his movements." He turned to the computer. "Oracle needs context."

Nadine moved to the screen, her expression intense.

"Oracle, this is Odin. Show me everything on Vivianne Valentine."

Data flooded the screen—surveillance photos, travel records, all leading back to Hong Kong.

"Oracle, search for Vivianne senior."

"Subject deceased...five years ago."

Nadine's frown deepened. "Her grandmother is listed as alive, but nobody's seen her in five years. I checked the grandmother's apartment—everything was pristine, maintained, but empty. No dust, no decay..."

"Like someone's keeping up appearances."

"Exactly. And the timing..." Nadine's eyes narrowed. "The grams disappears right when our jewel thief emerges. What if she didn't just disappear? But why wait? Unless...Holy shit. She's not watching for security patterns. She's watching for Sonya."

"Sonya moved out years ago. The only woman in that house now is—"

"She thinks Lara is Sonya."

Before I could process the words, Liam was already moving, racing toward his family with Nadine close behind.

13

KIERAN

She broke into *Lara's* house.

That was enough to set me off.

I had seen her photo in passing, but in real life the moment the words left my mouth I regretted it.

Fucking Christ.

She's gorgeous.

We had a team on her in a second after Nadine took her out. I felt off the moment I was in the house and hauling a passed out little lady to Titan Chicago.

Vivianne Valentine.

Too polished.

Too put-together.

Too not-for-me. Nah. Lara was my thing. Not girls like Vivianne.

Thieves with no moral compass on breaking into my home which was confusing as fuck for me.

I wasn't sure who the fuck gave her shit intel or how Liam fucking knew—then again—Liam always knew where Lara was concerned.

Liam was always aware of when his wife was in danger or uncomfortable and the moment that shit happened, Liam leapt into action. And me?

I got saddled with this lady.

And I had other plans and I had to admit, even if I was aware of how pretty she was. She was just another pretty face in the crowd to me now threatening my family.

I got women.

I got plenty of women.

I didn't need another one. Especially not when that woman made Luna cry. Not happening.

I was in Titan Tower in the heart of the city now rushing there with my fucking team. All of them grim-faced. Some of them with Liam making sure Lara and Luna were protected. Because nobody thought Lara out of all people would be attacked.

And now that they had?

Guns out.

Fun's over.

Imposing and towering, the entire fortress was owned by Reed Whittaker under the O'Hara's.

Imposing and towering, the entire fortress was owned by Reed Whittaker under the O'Haras. I followed Gideon Walsh—all six-feet-five-inches of pure shark teeth and muscle. Strapped with weapons and gear, he was menacing in the mood he was in.

I was in a *mood* too. But not entirely the kind my team would expect.

Every step I took, I felt my blood boiling at the idea of losing my goddaughter, and I adjusted my jacket, feeling my temper rising at the idea of anything happening under my roof. But underneath that rage was something else—anticipation. The kind that made my skin feel too tight.

To my left and right, flanking my every fucking step, were Tierian Hunter and Christian Lockwood, both livid.

"What did the Blake lady say in New York?"

"Over a painting for sure, but Teo took the painting to Nash Group with Sonya's. It's a map behind it."

Archer Vander had his tablet out, reading the email from the lady at Sotheby's who worked at the MET.

For some reason, this girl's intel led her to me. And despite everything, despite the threat she represented, I found myself wondering what it would be like to have those sharp eyes focused on me with something other than defiance.

What the fuck is wrong with you?

Vivianne Valentine had intel to break into Liam Sullivan's home? For who? Why? I was so fucking confused. Wasn't she looking for Sonya?

I didn't get it. She should've broken into my home. Should've come straight to me instead of threatening my family.

Should've given me a reason to get my hands on her that didn't involve restraints and interrogation rooms.

Jesus Christ, get it together.

Who the fuck was giving out messed-up intel? And who the fuck did I need to kill to get this shit fixed?

"Send out a team to Teo," I told Archer. "And find out what that map on the back of the painting is."

Nadine was gunning to kill her, what with everything happening to Josh.

And me? I wasn't about to let her have that satisfaction.

Nah. *Fuck that.*

Because despite everything—despite the threat, despite the chaos she'd brought into our lives—I wanted to be the one to break Vivianne Valentine down. Wanted to see what was underneath all that polish and planning.

Wanted to find out if she tasted as dangerous as she looked.

Aidan's gonna find out. Bombs are gonna blow up. If people so much as breathe wrong and interrupt his night with his wife—heads will roll in every city.

Instead, I wanted to talk to her about her existence.

Truth be told, I wanted to obliterate it from the face of the planet—but not before I figured out why every instinct I had was telling me to get closer instead of further away.

Vivianne Valentine who?

To put it nicely.

And I knew she was pretending, wasn't really passed out. The slight tension in her shoulders, the way her breathing was just a little too controlled. But I wasn't that nasty. I'd let it rock until she woke the fuck up.

Until she opened those eyes and looked at me like I was either her salvation or her destruction.

And then I'd flay her shitty career alive.

After I figured out why the thought of having her completely at my mercy was doing things to me that had nothing to do with justice.

I'd let the Chicago Titans handle her.

For now? I wanted to rip into someone else.

Someone who wouldn't make me question whether I wanted to destroy them or devour them.

So I went downtown with my guys to find out what the fuck was going on tonight. I was in a *mood*—the kind that came from wanting something I had no business wanting.

And I needed to lay into someone before I did something *stupid*.

Like wonder what Vivianne Valentine would sound like saying my name.

Whispering it.

Moaning it.

Crying it.

And then screaming it.

Nah.

That would not do.

14

KIERAN / VIVIANNE

I HAD TO GO TO NEW YORK WITH HER. TO THE METROPOLITAN.

One, the little thief in my life wanted two paintings that my family had. Two, I hadn't said much to her in a long time.

I barely had conversations with her, juggling my family.

Killian and Nisha had another baby. A third one to add to their brood. And then Aidan and Sonya wanted another baby.

And then everyone in Titan New York was having kids.

I was in charge of expanding Titan Chicago. And while this shit show happened with Vivianne, Gideon Walsh, a hire from Liam Sullivan was expanding Titan Miami.

With Talon.

Fuck my life.

That was another branch of Titan we had acquired and they were something else.

That was the direction I went to with Nash Group getting a hold of the CEO Natasha Nash. And I went to her husband, my old friend, Matteo DuPont.

Nash Group was in charge of art antiquities. Insurance. Security teams. And Talon. The big black-ops group that Thierry ran under Titan.

Gideon Walsh.

Nash Group says both paintings are in a vault under the MET

And the back?

The map leads them to Cape Verde

No shit

To the fucking Talon compound

No fucking way

Shut the fuck up

I sat up straighter. The map on the back of the paintings led to the Talon compound?

Does that mean the treasure doesn't belong to your little thief?

Or to the Nash's?

It belongs to Talon

And that girl has no idea

I have no problem crushing her spirit after her little stealth attack on Luna

No fucking problem whatsoever

Reina can take out her brother

I paused.
Take out her brother and then what?
What did I get from that?

Anything in the cards for him?

School

Scholarships

Money

74

Nothing much

She was going to buy him a new place to live

Kill it

Done

Liam's taking care of it

Reina?

Keep an eye on the kid.

We already know the treasure belongs to Nash

I don't give a shit about anything else

I'll get that handled

As I was texting him though I heard the clatter before I could do anything about it.

Fuck me.

It wasn't my choice to have her stay with me.

No. It was my brother's and I didn't argue because I knew better. I did. Keeping an eye on her here was good. Plus, we had guards.

But she did walk around.

It had been a week since the break-in. And I was still juggling multiple jobs and I hadn't gotten around to figuring out what I wanted to do with her.

I was confused by her.

I was.

I was thinking about what to do. How to do it. And why it mattered to me so much when I saw her in passing.

And why she got under my skin.

I blamed her eyes.

I knew her.

I had to right?

Why the fuck else would I stop?

I found two frozen tiny figures in real time glancing at me and then each other.

And one little thief staring at me gaping with her anklet, over-sized t-shirt, and socks on.

"Uhhh, sorry about that. They were in here when I came in."

My eyes darted over to my find my god-daughter and the enormous cat of the house staring down at a can of tuna on the ground.

Oh. *Fuck*. Me.

Ever since I got this fucking cat he ate everything in sight.

Everything.

And Luna was responsible for being the thief that snuck into the pantry with him and stole cans of tuna for him and fed him in her room.

And I didn't know and neither did Lara or Liam until recently.

The *cat* had gotten a tiny little step ladder, pushed it against the counter and had Luna climb up. And with her little fingers, she grabbed the tuna can, and was trying to feed him.

She just couldn't get down with the tuna in her hands.

So she was frozen.

And then her entire face contorted as Cheddar—that little shit —tore off into the house leaving her there.

"Oh snap, don't cry." I went to grab her and set her down, while putting the ladder away.

Luna began wailing at the top of her lungs.

"Nonono, they're gonna think I hit you or some shit—shoot, I mean I'm sorry, I'm not good at this—" she broke off realizing she was wailing louder and her mother was probably gonna come running.

I quickly went over to the entrance of the kitchen as and Liam emerged.

Liam went to Luna immediately his brows drawn.

"I didn't do anything—" she quickly explained what I saw and frowned at the tuna cans.

Why would she? Nobody blamed her. I barely said a fucking word which was unlike me because even if I liked her—I was juggling too much.

"*Munequita*," Liam lifted her into his arms. "Did you take the tuna?"

She shook her head into his neck.

"She's lying," I said protective and wondering if they'd blame me for making her cry.

They already blamed me for Mamie's death, they might blame me for her. I didn't trust the O'Hara's to invent things with me. Not with the anklet as a firm reminder of where I stood in their lives.

Another criminal.

Another job.

"She's got a habit of stealing for Cheddar, princess. We talked about this."

He looked nonchalant as he walked over to Luna who had quieted and hid into her father's neck.

I knew he was her father because they had the same eyes. And Liam smirked watching who picked up the tuna.

"I can't talk to the cat but I can talk to you, do you want Cheddar to live forever? Until you're older?"

She nodded sniffling and Liam snuggled her to him. She looked tiny compared to her father.

He smiled down at her. "I feed Cheddar twice a day, princess. Just two times." He held up a hand. "You cannot feed Cheddar unless Unca is there, okay?"

"But...but...but..."

"Slowly, shortcake," Liam muttered down to her.

"But he hungry," Luna tried with big eyes.

Kieran grinned down at her. "I know, princess. But we want Cheddar to be healthy. I already fed him. He is not hungry right now. He's a little—bad word. He's been a bad kitty."

"Bad kitty."

"Exactly," Kieran adjusted her little bow straightening it.

"All better?" Liam asked her with a proud smile and she nodded.

"Papi, bad kitty."

Liam smirked. "He's...clever. But no need to cry, *munequita*. It's okay, you have to tell Papi and Uncle the truth, okay? Did you try and take the tuna?"

Vivianne

"Luna's sick, we can't go right now to New York."

That was what I heard. Kieran O'Hara was for some reason helping me figure out where the second painting was. For someone who was a mobster he was interested more in the idea of the painting—then the gold behind it?

I didn't buy it for a second.

No I didn't really trust him but I couldn't deny he was getting under my skin.

"What?" I sat up more shocked he was stopping the entire fucking trip because of his god-child than anything else.

"We are not going, because Luna is sick," he repeated. "I need to go over there to make sure Lara and Liam aren't stretched thin and they get breaks. Stay here and don't try anything. Devlin and the security team are downstairs and they have their eyes on you."

I was left gaping with my mouth opening and closing as he said it and left.

Like I wasn't stunned fucking O'Hara was leaving me to my devices.

Over his god child.

Looks like the king of hell did have a heart and she was two feet tall with a binky and a marker in hand. I got the feeling would reschedule everything for his family.

And he did.

While he was gone I explored the O'Hara mansion. All of it.

As in from top to bottom, I went through most of the rooms. Some were locked. Killian's definitely locked with his name on it.

Instead, I found myself settling on the library where I found a few family photos on his desk.

"Happy families and all," I looked at the three brother's.

Killian's stoic cool expression.

Aidan's smirk casual and laid back. grinning ear to ear next to them making my heart skip a beat looking younger than ever.

But it was the girls in the photos that made me pause.

Killian's one arm held a little girl who was staring at him, in his other arm was a woman with raven hair and deep dark eyes.

Olive toned skin and she was hands down the prettiest woman ever.

She held another little girl who looked like her in her arms.

"A happy family."

Because Aidan looked the same. He grinned holding onto one of the twin girls and Sonya had looped her arms around both brother's.

I didn't know who took the photo but it captured all of their personalties well enough.

I snooped around finding Luna's toys, photos of her in all stages, Liam and Lara holding her, Lara and . A life without me. A normal one.

I wandered finding a book to read and roaming like a ghost.

I was trapped here, I might as well make the most of it.

15

VIVIANNE

WAKING UP AT A HOLDING CELL AT FOUR A.M WAS NOT THE WAKE UP call anyone wanted. Was I in and out?

Yes.

Did I want to be?

No.

Not with five men in the other side of the cell quietly on their phones.

I couldn't run. But I thought about it.

But how?

I was spooked to say the least. And I was lying down, feeling the panic swell in my chest. The unease in my stomach.

My chest tightening with apprehension.

Tall and imposing, one of the blonde guys stood up coming over to me with a booted foot looking scarier than I could've fathomed.

"Lockwood, make sure she doesn't leave without a tracker."

A deeper voice cut through the air menacing and I was suddenly aware of myself getting into more trouble than I could handle.

I thought I'd just spook one of the ladies of the manor and I don't know why Greenie gave me that address.

I thought I'd be breaking into Matteo DuPont's house.

Not someone named Liam O'Hara.

I think I got something wrong here.

Did Greenie set me up?

The thought careened into my head like a miniature rocket.

And then bounced around a bit without exploding, making me feel a headache coming on.

I didn't mean to attack one of their own but I was terrified he was gonna come after me.

And he would've.

And I had to stay alive for my family. For Erik. Erik's dreams weren't about to be wasted.

I just had to stay quiet to find my way out. And then the big scary blonde, towering over me closer than the others opened the door.

"Let's go, Miss."

I didn't say a word.

This was not how I chalked up this whole thing.

I thought Liam would have the painting. I thought I'd get in and out. Not find a little lady there. My intel was bad.

It was wrong.

Greenie fucked me over?

And now I was busted by a group of guys that only wanted God knows what with me.

His friend was holding an anklet. Like a tracking anklet. Fuck my life.

"You a Fed?"

He didn't say a word.

All of them looked miserable as he walked up into the cell. The crick in my neck was aching more as I straightened up from where I was laying.

And I straightened some more as he came in. Stone-faced and threatening I just stopped breathing as he got to his knees quickly and snapped it on me.

I didn't even have time to scramble back.

Instead I just sat there as he walked back out.

"Boss wants her in the manor."

I had no idea what was going on but it didn't matter I was in so much fucking trouble.

"Hey, am I gonna be let out of this joint?"

"No." A dark-haired man standing at close to six-five maybe, covered with knuckle tattoos. "You're being held here for the next few days under surveillance for your crimes against Titan."

I swallowed. Titan?

Hold up.

Hold the fucking phone.

I didn't commit any crimes against Titan.

I was after a painting.

"Is this a joke?"

"Lady, does it look like we're joking," a dark-haired man with messy hair and wicked brown-eyes glanced up at me, more annoyed than angry. "What the fuck were you even thinking?"

And I didn't know what to say since I didn't get read my rights.

No, a smaller woman named Reina Lawless showed up to do my fingerprints and talk to me about how fucked I was politely of course.

And then she put me back into the holding cell.

A DAMN TRACKING DEVICE.

That's what gave me.

All six-feet three inches of O'Hara with amber eyes watched me from across the cell, his pitch black tactical gear making him look like death personified.

Behind him, Nadine Forrester leaned against the wall, her dark eyes never leaving me.

The two of them made quite the picture—beauty and danger wrapped in Titan's colors.

He didn't like me.

The feeling was mutual.

Even handcuffed and bleeding, I couldn't help noticing how the devil himself looked in the fluorescent lighting—chocolate brown hair falling over those amber eyes, jawline sharp enough to cut glass.

The motherfucker was handsome as sin.

But I knew he was the king of hell.

I had crossed into his domain without thinking twice and now I realized—I should've thought twice. Should've. Could've. Would've.

But now I fucked up. I didn't know about the O'Hara family reputation like that until I got caught by them.

I just knew over the last few years there was a buyer—a family—silently taking over all of Chicago. All of it.

As in I couldn't fucking move a fucking muscle without them knowing. My every breath was being monitored.

They had a clinic I got taken to and one of the doctor's Colton Wells checked me in and out.

Introducing himself as a resident, I ended up being carted past a few people with two guards and he knew them.

Titan Chicago apparently had a team up here in this ward in the hospital.

He was with Dusan Voronov.

Christian Lockwood, a taller blonde man with clean cut hair, at six-three muscled up and armed to the teeth and his counterpart, Archer Vander was a golden-haired man who wore a ball cap most of the time covering his eyes in black.

Even indoors.

Dressed in all black with a gold trim on their "uniform" the Titan Chicago team wasn't the same as the New York team.

I didn't know what his deal was but his eyes were the shade of azure. Bluer than anything I'd ever seen.

And on me with annoyance.

He didn't want to be here babysitting me.

Everyone seemed short-tempered with me. I had been introduced to a woman named Carina Kindcaide who was former FBI and Intelligence.

Now, she worked IT for Chicago Titan.

The entire damn underworld knew about the O'Hara family's reputation.

I thought Aidan was still in power—that was the thing about the O'Haras I was starting to understand.

They never actually told anyone their plans or what was going to happen.

I don't even know what I do the rest of the day.

Or the unfinished conversations nobody wanted to have with me.

I was currently being baby-sitted on by Kieran fucking O'Hara for attacking his family.

And according to them—I should've been grateful I wasn't in jail.

My full scholarship came through for next year.

And I think I met a girl the same day.

A cute girl.

> No shit?

> How?

> And what girl? Here I thought you were as sexual as a plant.

Ha. Ha. Real funny, sis. I like girls.

And shes a student here at Kingston. She's hot.

She's got some older brother who works out in Chicago but shes dope af

Some special grant money the school got, this fucking means I don't need to get a job, whatever money I have on the side I can keep.

> Sweet.

> What's her name?

Renata. I think. She has a nickname.

Got this whole 'quiet but could ruin your life' vibe.

She's got an older brother who works out in Chicago—some finance job, I think.

Protective as hell, but she's dope af.

sounds like a girl who drinks espresso with no sugar

And judges people for using plastic straws

Meanie

Not quite

Are you sure shes good?

What about her brother?

Do you need help?

If he says some shit to you let me know

AND NOW I WAS OFFICIALLY HELD HOSTAGE BY THE O'HARA syndicate even if I wanted to just find my painting.

So I began working in secret to get there.

And I wasn't going to tell Kieran O'Hara anything.

I was plotting my escape more than my victories.

16

KIERAN

I'm upset you're not coming.

THAT WAS THE TEXT I GOT FROM NISHA.

Having sisters-in-law meant they checked up on you all the time.

Nisha and Sonya combined meant I was always taken care of—sometimes whether I wanted it or not.

While my mind was racing with the thoughts of my current problem not being a problem.

Vivianne Valentine was in her early twenties—struggling to make her ends meet and she was getting under my skin. Because she never asked for anything. She never did anything. She was quiet.

We tracked her cell phone and her text messages out to a few people. But overall?

She wasn't anything I saw coming.

She was beautiful.

Not at all annoying. Soft-spoken. Quiet. And she kept to herself and I was aware Teo, one of my buddies dropping off the painting to Nash Group—and that was the end of it.

But for some reason she was still chasing it.

Aidan's advice was to see a game out. Full-play.

Killian would crush things by the first issue. Aidan would let it play out to make people squirm to see where they would go. How far they were willing to go.

He wanted to know who was after him, his family, his proverbial crown, his home—and worse—Luna?

We didn't know.

And me?

I didn't know what to do or why my brother was asking me to see this through to the end.

It wasn't bad enough she broke into the house. Even if we had the two paintings—I didn't tell her.

I didn't say a word.

I wanted to see where she was going, and why, and how far she was willing to go to get her hands on the map. The treasure.

The coins. I wasn't sure but I assumed it was treasure.

Juggling everything else in my life was hard enough.

I didn't know why she did why she did.

I tried to get the girls to talk to her not the guys and she said next to nothing to everyone.

No attitude.

Just quiet responses and monotonous around me.

I didn't talk to her. But I wanted to.

She was too quiet.

I had questions.

She had answers.

But nobody could get them.

And I suspected she had a secret phone.

> Jewel thief in house.

> Need extra hands to manage her.

> I also don't feel comfortable with the entire thing.

> Is Killian gonna bring the girls to see me when I'm in the city?

He wants to he says I can't see you so I'll be sending food

> I hate all this

She would. Nisha didn't feel comfortable with any of this.
Not the treasure part.
The whole helping out a thief part.

> What's she like?
>
> Your new roommate.
>
> A real thief huh? That sounds fun.

> It is until you realize she needs to be babysat 24/7

> Welcome to motherhood

I laughed outright when I read that.
I got a text from Killian immediately after that one.

> Stop texting Nisha sad shit, motherfucker

I rolled my eyes.

> Leave it to you to be over protective

But that's what we did, wasn't it? Protected what was ours.
Even if sometimes that meant protecting people from themselves.
I didn't see her in her room, but it said she was in the house.
I was walking out of the bedroom and I stopped in my tracks at
the sight of her on her knees on the ground and for a moment I
would've asked her if she was okay.
If she was all right.
And all the words stopped in my tracks at the sight of her
touching herself.
Her headphones on and phone lying there as she thrust her
fingers into her body, her mouth opened in a little O.
I blinked a little gaping at the sight of her biting her lip now and
I knew the moment she peaked.

The way she fell over and worked her body.

Desperate.

Hungry.

Writhing.

Fuck.

~

Did I wanna leave Chicago?

No.

I didn't want to go to New York.

I didn't want to interact with anyone. I wanted to stay curled into my nest at the mansion and not move.

But being an adult and being a boss meant doing that shit.

I fucking hated it.

We landed in Newark and made our way into the city off the private plane.

Aidan had one he used all the time and it was much easier than traveling with anyone else.

It also helped if you had a passenger on board wearing a tracking anklet that you at the minimum were allowed privacy.

"Where are we going?" She grumbled half asleep.

"Hotel Primrose," I explained. "Sonya owns it."

And knowing both of my sister-in-laws, the moment I checked in, Nisha would send over plenty of food and Sonya wouldn't let me starve.

Both of them were the polar opposite of my siblings and somehow it made sense.

Nisha filled Killian's life with enough love to make him tattoo hearts his daughters drew on his wrist, and Sonya held Aidan together while he explored what the fuck he was trying to do at thirty fucking years old.

"What do you brother's do?"

"A little bit of this, a little bit of that," I grinned at her frown. "What?"

"Why do you talk like someone with secrets?"

89

"The same reason you're in an ankle bracelet." I motioned to it. "It's all business."

I got the feeling it would make her look softer and less mean.

I grinned at that and she scowled at me more.

"Are you always this annoying?"

"You held my sister at gunpoint," I reminded her lightly.

Liam wasn't my brother per se, but Lara was every bit my family. I always considered her an extension of us.

She was quiet the entire way and I thought like me, she might be processing her half of the painting of the Storm, reuniting with the only other half in existence. The real half.

Sonya had it and now Aidan would bring it to the Primrose.

I knew Titan merged with the other unit and now they were a joint operations group.

We made it into the city and I saw Vivianne looking around.

"You ever been here?"

"I have, but only on jobs. Not to sightsee," she murmured. She was always distracted and I was too busy admiring her hair.

The curve of her cheek.

The way she smiled a little at the ceiling, every tiny little ornament, like she saw more than everybody else.

I liked that about her.

Did I like Vivianne Valentine?

Not exactly.

But she was growing on me. It had been a few weeks that Vivianne had been in my life. And I initially thought she was going to be a problem.

But she wasn't.

No, the only problem was that she was getting under my skin and I didn't know what to do about it.

At the Primrose, I took our keys to the suite at the top.

Vivianne was still glancing around the place.

"Only one room?" She frowned.

"Relax, I got us two beds."

I heard her muttering about like she'd wanna sleep with me anyway. I smirked. Right. Like she didn't want to.

She reminded me of the things I didn't know how to confront.

The weight of choices I never wanted to make, of cages gilded in family obligation.

Looking out over Manhattan's glittering skyline, I could almost hear Cormac's voice.

A son's duty is to family first.

It's been fucking days since the incident.

My father had believed in duty right up until the end, even as his fists taught us what happened to sons who questioned it.

I'd left this city five years ago when Aidan needed me in Chicago. Another choice that wasn't really a choice.

Trade one skyline for another, one prison for a bigger one.

But at least in Chicago, I could protect them—Aidan, Killian, their families. Build something that wasn't founded on our father's brutality.

"Foods coming," I said, not looking directly at Vivianne.

Her reflection in the window reminded me too much of myself at that age—haunted eyes, shoulders bent under invisible weights.

"Aidan will be here in an hour."

"You trust me to meet your brother?" She perched on the edge of one bed, as far from me as possible.

Like a bird ready to take flight at the first sign of danger. I knew that instinct. Had lived it under Cormac's roof.

"I trust the anklet. And I trust that you're smart enough to know what happens if you try anything."

The words came out harder than intended, an echo of my father that made me want to wash my mouth out.

"I'm not going to hurt anyone else."

I studied her reflection, this woman who'd do anything to protect her brother.

Who'd built her own gilded cage of lies and sacrifice.

Maybe that's why I couldn't bring myself to be as cruel as I should be. I recognized too much in her desperate choices.

The city lights blurred together, past and present merging.

"I know you won't," I said finally, softer than before. "You're not the monster in this story, Vivi. Neither of us are. We're just trying to protect what's ours."

17

KIERAN

"Why do you steal?"

The question came out before I could stop it, genuine curiosity breaking through my usual control.

She met my eyes in the window's reflection, and for a moment, I saw understanding flash there. Recognition of shared wounds, of choices that weren't choices, of cages we'd built ourselves.

She stiffened, but her eyes stayed locked with mine in the glass. "Because I have to."

"No," I turned to face her directly. "You don't. That's the lie we tell ourselves. There are always choices."

"Really?" Her laugh was bitter coffee, dark and biting. "Then why do you kill people?"

The question should have angered me. Instead, I felt my lips curve into a humorless smile. "Because I have to."

"No," she threw my words back at me, standing now. "You don't. That's the lie you tell yourself."

We stood there, the truth hanging between us like smoke—both of us hiding behind our supposed lack of choices, both of us knowing better.

"Maybe," I said finally. "We're both just too scared to make different ones."

Her hand went to her necklace again, but this time it seemed less like a tell and more like a lifeline. "Different choices mean different risks."

"Different failures."

"Different losses."

In the window's reflection, her eyes found mine. For a heartbeat, I watched something crack open in her expression—recognition, maybe.

The look of someone who'd seen their own ghost walking around in someone else's skin.

Her shoulders went rigid, but she didn't look away from our mirrored images in the glass. "What kind of question is that?"

"An honest one."

"Honest." She turned the word over like it tasted foreign. "From a man who kills people for a living."

The accusation should have made me defensive.

Should have reminded me why keeping distance was safer for both of us.

Instead, I found myself turning away from the window to face her directly.

"That's not an answer."

"Because I have to." The words came out flat, rehearsed.

A script she'd been reciting so long she almost believed it.

"No." I kept my voice level, matter-of-fact. "You don't."

Her laugh was sharp enough to draw blood. "Really? Then enlighten me about all these magical choices I apparently have."

"The same ones I have when I pull a trigger."

That stopped her.

She studied my face, looking for the trap, the manipulation. When she didn't find it, something shifted in her posture—guard dropping just enough to let truth slip through.

"So why do you?" Her voice was quieter now, genuinely curious. "Kill people, I mean."

I could have deflected. Should have. Could have reminded her that she was the prisoner here, that I didn't owe her explanations or confessions.

Instead, I heard myself say. "Because it's easier than the alternative."

"Which is?"

"Living with what happens when I don't."

She nodded slowly, like I'd finally said something that made sense. "There it is."

"There what is?"

"The real answer." She moved closer, close enough that I could see the gold flecks in her dark eyes. "It's not because we have to. It's because we can't live with the consequences of not doing it."

The truth sat between us, heavy and unwelcome.

I'd spent years telling myself I had no choice, that family obligation and circumstances had painted me into a corner.

But she was right—every trigger I'd pulled, every life I'd taken, had been a choice.

A choice to protect what mattered to me, even if it meant becoming something I hated.

"Different choices," I said slowly.

"Different consequences." Her fingers found her necklace, worrying the chain. "Different people we'd have to become."

"Different people we'd have to watch suffer."

She was close enough now that I could smell her shampoo, see the tiny scar above her left eyebrow.

Close enough to notice the way her pulse jumped in her throat when she whispered. "What if we're not strong enough to be different people?"

Asking it meant admitting that maybe, just maybe, we both wanted to try.

To be better.

To be different.

18

KIERAN

It was raining when we ran into the hotel.

Vivianne let out a breathless, embarrassed laugh—half apology, half delight—as she pushed her wet hair out of her face, cheeks flushed from the cold and the sprint.

I shook out the umbrella corralling her into the elevator and biting back my own laughter as I held onto our takeout bags.

We should've just ordered in.

That had been the plan, hadn't it? Stay in.

Avoid the cabin fever that had been eating away at the both of us, gnawing at nerves and patience.

But somewhere between pacing the suite and the way Vivianne kept walking around in just a towel, her bare shoulders still glistening from the shower, I'd lost the thread of common sense.

Who knew?

I ended up carting back the Greek food after realizing cabin fever was very real.

It was so fucking real it was eating at my insides enough to know that I was on edge.

One horny edge of a ledge that I couldn't climb down from.

Fuck my life.

And we were going to claw each other's eyes out.

Or worse.

Fuck it out until I could taste her on my tongue all the time and never let her go.

I was going to jump her bones with the way I felt about her showering in the same room and coming out with a towel on all modest and shit.

Vivianne watched the oddest shows and I walked in on her all the time flopped on my couch, half-asleep, and out of it.

She would munch on m&ms and smuggle takeout boxes of odd Korean food the housekeeper would find.

And then she'd pass out.

And I'd carry her back to her room and she'd wake up and we'd work together on the map.

I carted her gently into the elevator and pressed our floor as four guys got in. Enormous and built like linebackers, they wore jackets for Astor U's Dark Knights.

But right behind them was two guys from Kingston Prep.

Absolutely the fuck not.

We were not going to do this shit here. Those guys and their rivalries were ruthless.

Even I was tracking them with a new New York Titan team.

Because they were always causing problems.

And right now? There was an assault case pending on a female student in Astor U for a guy from Kingston Prep and that made folks lose their shit.

But I didn't wanna start a fucking fight so I tucked Vivi into my side.

I could barely get into the room. Barely make it through the door before I was on her.

I drove into Vivianne with little finesse. I told myself to control myself better whenever I was with her.

But I couldn't.

I snapped my hips into her, driving deeper with every inch, as she squirmed under me a tiny bit. Her hands gripped my shirt.

"Come on, little thief, let me in."

Her eyes glazed over a little, lashes fluttering halfway as her mouth opened in a little o.

"I'm gonna love you right, all night, all day, every single day—"
and I held back.

Because if I said too much?

She might get scared and run faster.

So I kept my fucking mouth shut. That's how I ran with it now.

Maybe when she got more comfortable I could talk to her.

Tell her that I'd be there for her. Hug her.

Be there for her.

But also?

Let her squirm on my face and lick that ache inside of her
better. But for now?

I'd be that guy.

This guy.

And that would be enough?

Absolutely not.

Absolutely.

Not.

She had no idea she was mine.

She just had an idea that she belonged to me in a way she hated.
Did I take off the anklet when she slept?

Yeah. I wasn't a fucking tool.

But now?

Now I wish I had more resolve to be better because I wanted to
devour her. Destroy her.

Love her. Stay with her forever.

But I knew for right now? I had to love her.

Love her right. Love her true to what I knew was the woman
under me?

Wasn't who she pretended to be. She wasn't the thief the world
knew her to be.

She was the sweetest thing in the world once you got her down
to it. And the kindest.

The one with the biggest heart.

And I got to love her.

"Is that better?"

She didn't say a word, eyes locking with mine, for a nanosecond. And she gasped into my mouth.

"Kieran—"

I paused. I wasn't halfway in yet.

I wasn't even halfway and she tightened around me and I sank in further.

A dark tight smile formed slowly as I sank in further.

Further.

I bit it back.

She couldn't say it. Couldn't tell me. And I couldn't be mean. No. She hadn't said a word.

And I knew she wanted to say plenty.

I just had to figure out how to get her to say it.

Just say it.

Just tell me what you want.

Come on, baby.

And she didn't say a word.

Instead, she gripped my arm and held on tighter and I sank in further.

My hand moved to her face to hold on and I shoved in the rest of the way and sealed my mouth over hers.

JesusfuckingChrist.

When was the last time she'd been with anyone?

How did I even ask that?

Usually I was articulate, but right now, I needed to not be articulate. But to make her feel safe and comfortable too. Not just like I was going to fuck her.

I'd fled to the street like an idiot. Greek food. Rain.

The ache of restraint riding shotgun the entire time.

She was killing me.

No, correction—we were going to kill each other. Slowly. Tension so sharp between us it had a sound.

Or worse.

We were going to snap and fuck the frustration out of each other until we broke the damn headboard—or something inside of us cracked wide open.

≈

I POUNDED DEEP INTO HER LOVING HER LITTLE WHIMPERS AND screams. Vivianne was sensitized beyond belief.

"That's it, baby. Give it to me. As many as you got."

She was going to lose her voice. It was going to hurt to walk. She was going to be sore.

And I would make it better. Take care of her. Run her a bath. Massage her hair.

Watch her squirm until she begged me to lick that pussy better. *Fuck.*

I pounded deep through it relishing the fluttering around my cock but aware that I kept going for her.

I wanted to come the moment Vivianne said she didn't have birth control. I was going to lose it. I had held myself back by an inch if not a mile. But I could only hold back for so long before the thinnest thread I was leaning against snapped. Fragmented. Shattered. Obliterated to pieces by a woman more devastating to me than my own reputation.

And now?

Inside of her? It took everything to not come but I knew I wanted to see her come apart. Over and over.

She was great without toys.

With toys. She was fucking explode.

Tied up and vibed within an inch. So *sensitive*. She came so fast. As she calmed down an animal noise followed and I just knew—

"Is that better, baby?"

I grinned looking down at her, panting, breathless, tear streaked face unable to see me.

"Good," I bent lower. "I love warming you up."

And then I grabbed the toy she'd missed earlier loving the way she didn't stir. She didn't move. Because she was mine.

And she knew who she belonged too.

"That's it, let go, baby, let it go, I got you."

19

VIVIANNE

I HAD A LOVE HATE RELATIONSHIP WITH FOOD.

Because I had gained weight in the last few years and I had gone from a size four to a size ten. And I wasn't happy with how every single day I looked at myself and I had to adjust myself in the mirror. The roll of my stomach, the cinch at my waist, the way my hips dipped—this new body was unfamiliar to me.

I picked at my food at best. And I didn't eat in public ever. I chose the worst pieces of meat for myself. Never ate more than enough for a toddler. And I never pressed the issue with a nutritionist or a doctor.

I never talked about it with anybody either.

And now I was paying for it since Kieran O'Hara looked at me hungrily like he knew my secrets. But he didn't. Did he? He couldn't.

He couldn't have guessed. But if he did?

I was going to lose it.

Lose it. The man was digging into every corner of my psyche more than I knew. And over time I was worried I might cave and do something worse than have sex with him.

But fall for him.

Lord knew, Erik would love him.

I gave everything to my brother, and if I went hungry he never knew. That was the game I played with myself for years. Give everything to Eric. Keep quiet. Swallow the ache.

Smile if anyone asked. Pretend I was full when I was breaking inside.

Every night my stomach grumbled. Rather than being bitter, I accepted it as a facet of my life. And I just moved on.

Shoved the hunger to the side and pushed it away so it wouldn't matter anymore much like everything else.

I used to think hunger was a kind of strength.

If I could ignore it, outlast it, bury it deep enough that it stopped clawing at me—I was winning.

Back then, food wasn't nourishment. It was guilt. It was shame. It was a plate I didn't think I deserved.

I'd pick at crusts, chew around bones, tell myself I wasn't hungry even when I was dizzy from it.

I made a habit of starving.

And not just my body.

Myself.

I starved myself of softness.

Of comfort. Of the simple, human right to be fed—without apology, without rationing joy down to crumbs.

But lately...things are different.

I still hesitate when someone puts a plate in front of me.

My instinct is to measure how much is *too much*, how much I can leave behind to feel in control. But something's shifted.

Maybe it's Kieran. Maybe it's me.

The other day, I ate without explaining myself.

There was no bargaining in my head. No math. No shame. I was hungry. And I ate. That was all.

And when I looked up, no one was judging me. No one was watching. No one flinched.

Least of all me.

It's not about the food. It never was.

It's about letting myself want. Letting myself need. Letting myself exist without apology.

And maybe tomorrow I'll pick at my plate again. Maybe I won't. But today—I fed myself.

On purpose.

And that's enough.

And around Kieran?

I couldn't do that. I couldn't do any of that.

I picked at fries, and he noticed.

I pushed meat to the edge of my plate, and he noticed.

I ate like a child trying to hide a secret, and he noticed.

"Why don't you eat..." Kieran's voice trailed off as he stared down at the gyro in front of him.

Pita bread, lamb, tzatziki sauce—too much. Too soft. Too layered.

The pita alone looked like a mountain.

I stared at it, daunted. I wanted the hummus—

God, I wanted the whole tub of it—but everything else felt like a chore. A battle I didn't have the strength to win.

"Eating isn't my favorite time of day," I said, quietly.

He looked up. "What is?"

"Twilight. Dawn."

He blinked, chewing slowly.

I liked the in-between hours.

The moments that didn't demand anything of me. The sunrise before the city woke up. The purple hush before everything ended.

Time felt softer then. Forgiving. Like I could exist without being watched or weighed down.

"What do you eat at twilight?" he asked.

"Tea. Cake."

Safe things. Sweet things. Tiny things.

Things I could break into pieces and still pretend I wasn't really eating.

His mouth curved as he bit into his lamb. Bastard. No one should look that good while eating.

It should've been illegal—the way his jaw worked, the way he didn't even think about it.

He just fed himself like he deserved to.

Meanwhile, I was still nibbling at crumbs like I hadn't earned the right to eat something whole.

Like every bite needed permission.

Kieran slid a tray toward me. "Try that with your hummus. It's good. I promise."

I stared at it.

Messy. Warm. A little too much. A little too generous.

My stomach growled—sharp and real and undeniable—and the anklet around my ankle blinked green.

Still tethered.

Still under surveillance.

Still a part of me that didn't know how to stop proving I could survive without needing anything.

But I looked at the plate again. At him.

And maybe for once, surviving didn't have to mean starving.

Maybe I could take a bite without explaining. Without feeling the anxiety of food and the pressure of eating. The pressure of every single bite. The pressure of every calorie. The pressure of not living up to the reputation I had built somehow irrationally surrounding my eating habits.

Maybe I could want something without guilt crawling up my throat.

I reached for the tray. Slowly. Carefully.

It was messy. It was too much. It's not enough.

Too fat. Too ugly. Too skinny. Too much.

Never enough. Not quite.

But for the first time in a long time, I wanted to taste something just because I could.

And that felt like something.

Not a breakthrough.

But a beginning.

"I have money," I said.

"I know. It's not a competition. I'm telling you to eat."

I reached for my phone instead.

"What are you doing?" he asked, frowning.

"Calling room service. I'm hungry as fuck—"

"You can just eat your food—"

"I can. And you can too."

I turned and caught him watching me, eyes wide, raven hair

spilling everywhere like he'd just walked out of a dream and wasn't ready to be seen.

"Calm down, woman. I'm hungry either way." I tapped through the menu. "I need protein. And if I eat a goddamn protein bar, Nisha's going to get some kind of mental mom alert and call me about it."

THE NEXT MORNING WAS WHEN MY REALITY SHATTERED INTO PIECES.
Shattered.
Completely.
I got a text from Greenie.

> Sorry about the fuck up with the O'Hara's
>
> I didn't mean to steer you wrong

Yes. He had.

> I have some news for you about the painting

> Which is

I cursed myself out before realizing what I had done.
I never told Kieran or the Titans I kept a burner phone.
Greenie had the number.
Greenie had contacted me.
Greenie didn't know I was in New York. And he had no fucking clue that I was with Kieran O'Hara at the Primrose.
And he had no fucking what the fuck I was hiding and he had no fucking clue about anything.
And now after weeks of giving me bad information, he was now texting me.
Major.
Red.
Flags.
And on top of all that?
What the fuck was I supposed to do? Tell Greenie or Kieran?

No, I was keeping secrets from everybody and I didn't want to tell anyone anything.

I just wanted to keep it myself and I didn't want anyone else to know about it.

No, nobody could know.

And now?

What the fuck did I tell Kieran?

I didn't trust Greenie or Kieran and I was risking it out here by my brother. My brother who was in harms way.

I had to maintain a facade of calm. Total calm.

And I contacted another associate I knew about.

I met Aria Steele from Greenie's connections in Downtown Chicago.

Someone who moved in the shadows—part of a group that did *this* for a living.

Private security, covert and discreet. A shadow network working under Nash Group's wings.

I figured if anyone could read between the lines, it'd be her.

I hit her up, careful not to reveal too much.

Mentioned Titan, the messages from Greenie.

She told me nothing. Or maybe she just couldn't.

But she gave me no answers.

Still, I sent her the texts.

Better to have a woman to talk to—someone who might understand the danger lurking beneath the words—than anyone else.

Even if trust was still miles away, it was a thread.

And sometimes, in this game, a thread was all you had.

He didn't text back.

Im outtie

No. I got info.

About your Mamie's painting

My heart paused. We were in New York. And as far as I was aware, Kieran wanted me to help find the second painting.

And tell him about the map on the back.

And tell him everything that I could.

Or you could run.

That little voice in the back of my mind was urging me to run. I didn't know Kieran or the Titans or if I could trust them.

I didn't know what to do.

Run from Kieran.

Run from the Titans.

Run from everything I didn't understand, everything I feared.

I didn't know who Kieran really was beneath the calm, beneath the strength.

I didn't know if the Titans were protectors...or something darker.

I didn't know if trust was a luxury I could afford.

All I knew was that the ground beneath me felt shaky—like stepping onto ice that might crack at any moment.

And I didn't know what to do.

Fear twisted in my gut, tight and cold.

I couldn't even formulate the words—What is it?

Before Greenie texted back.

Your painting is a fake

I had it checked out

Its a fraud

And just like that everything I had worked so hard for came crashing to a halt.

I couldn't breathe.

I backed away before I even realized I was moving. My heel hit the doorframe, and then I was outside, feet hitting pavement, heartbeat pounding in my throat like it wanted out.

I ran.

Past the alley. Past the streetlights.

Didn't matter where. I just needed *away*.

Because I couldn't handle the way he looked at me like I was something *worth saving*.

I didn't trust it.

Didn't trust *him*.

And worst of all—I didn't trust myself to stay.

20

KIERAN

SHE RAN.

Of course she did.

Of course she fucking did.

I wasn't in there long. Just a minute.

A breath.

leaned on the sink and stared at my reflection like it had answers.

Like maybe the man in the mirror could explain what the hell I was doing—how I'd gone from running operations to watching a girl eat fries like it was a miracle.

My knuckles pressed into the edge of the counter, grounding myself.

I didn't feel steady. Not around her. Vivianne had eaten.

Just a little. A few bites, maybe. But she *ate*. That alone felt like a fucking victory. A fragile, ridiculous, beautiful victory.

She didn't argue. Didn't snap at me.

Didn't flinch when I pushed the plate closer.

She just...sat there.

Quiet. Cautious.

But present.

It was more than I'd ever asked for.

And something in me softened in the space she left open.

Something I'd kept locked down for a long time.

God, I wanted to believe it meant something.

That she wasn't just enduring the moment—

That she might actually *want* to be there.

With me.

Not because she had to.

Not because she was trapped.

But because she was starting to trust.

Me.

Us.

Anything.

I let out a slow, unsteady breath. Turned off the tap. I told myself not to want too much. Not to expect too much.

But still—hope was a hell of a thing. It blooms even in war zones. I opened the door. And stopped.

The room was too quiet. Too still. Her energy—always vibrating, always alert—was gone. My pulse kicked up, hard and fast.

The kind of shift that comes right before everything goes to hell. A sixth sense.

A warning. One I knew too well.

She was gone. And something inside me—something I didn't want to name—began to crack. Like the silence had weight. I stepped out.

The chair was empty. Her coat was gone.

The window cracked open, curtain dancing like it was mocking me. And the air—it still smelled like her. My chest squeezed tight. She ran.

Not because I believed in fairytales. I knew better.

But something about the way she looked at me before I walked into that bathroom—calmer, less guarded, like she was finally letting me be near her—I thought we'd turned a corner.

Clearly, I was wrong.

I stepped into the hallway, my boots already hitting the tile too fast.

My pulse was a hammer. Not panic. Not yet.

But that instinct was there, and it was loud.

I threw the front door open and hit the street.

New York was buzzing—traffic, noise, too many people.

None of it mattered.

I scanned every face. Every figure. Every flick of dark hair that might be hers.

She couldn't have gotten far. Not barefoot. Not in this wind.

Not with her thighs still shaking from how tightly she'd been wound sitting across from me.

I turned right. Then sharp left.

The bodega's neon sign glared like a warning.

She was fast—she always had been.

I called her name.

Nothing.

I picked up speed. Not running, not yet, but close.

I didn't chase her because I thought I could fix her.

I chased her because she needed to know I wasn't afraid of the mess.

I wasn't afraid of the baggage, the silence, the walls she threw up every time I got close.

I wasn't afraid of the panic in her eyes when I looked at her too long, like I might see something she wasn't ready to admit.

I wanted her anyway.

The way she closed up when someone got too close.

The way she froze when kindness came without conditions.

The way she pushed the plate of food toward me like she didn't think she deserved it.

And yeah, I wanted her in other ways too.

The way her breath caught when I leaned in.

The way her legs crossed tighter like she didn't trust her body to behave.

The tension in her shoulders, begging for release even if her mouth refused to ask for it.

I wasn't just chasing her because I cared.

I was chasing her because I *felt* her.

Every flicker of her hesitation. Every damn pull between us.

I didn't need her to be perfect.

I just needed her to *stay*.

And if I had to run this city down to find her, I would.

But because I couldn't let her leave thinking I didn't give a damn.

Because she didn't get to vanish with my name still on her lips and my hands still carrying the heat of her.

Because I *wanted* her.

Not just her sweetness. Not just the shadows.

I wanted all of her.

Even the wild parts.

Especially the ones that made her run.

She didn't scare me.

Not the broken parts.

Not the walls.

Not even the fact that half the time I wanted to pin her to the nearest surface and the other half I just wanted to hold her until she stopped shaking.

Because I'd chase her every damn time.

And when I caught her—

I was going to remind her why she should've stayed.

She's got a place in Brooklyn

It's under the name Aria Steele

Sound familiar?

Thank fuck for T

Tell me about it

Thats who she went to

She doesn't know about Reina or anything but Aria said she knows the painting is fake

Lets keep it that way

I gotta go find her

THE BUILDING LOOKED EMPTY FROM THE STREET—A FADING SIGN FOR a photography collective no one remembered anymore, its windows covered in dust and old paint, the kind of place people walked past without seeing.

But I saw her.

A flicker of movement on the third floor. A shadow drawn in light.

I took the stairs two at a time, boots heavy on the concrete, heart louder than it should've been. She'd run here.

Not to vanish—To *breathe.*

The door creaked as I pushed it open. Dust hung thick in the air, lit up by a single crack of moonlight bleeding through the broken skylight.

The walls were stained with old paint. Canvases leaned crooked in the corners.

And I knew. I just fucking knew she was here.

The scent of night-blooming jasmines and gardenias came through the place and all my anger bled out of me.

I didn't even know what to do right now other than wrangle her back to the hotel room.

She knew I was there. And I didn't say a damn thing.

I stepped inside, slow, careful—like she was a storm and I was trying not to get struck.

My eyes dragged over her, cataloguing every detail.

Not for weakness—for the ache I hadn't realized I'd been carrying until I saw her like this.

I didn't even know what the hell to do right now—other than get her back to the hotel, back to somewhere warm, somewhere safe.

Somewhere that didn't feel like this.

But even that felt impossible.

Because she wasn't just hiding.

She was *breaking.*

And I couldn't fix it.

Couldn't touch it.

Couldn't touch *her*—not yet.

She knew I was there.

I felt it in the stillness of her shoulders, the way her breath caught like she was holding the whole moment hostage.

And I didn't say a damn thing.

I stepped inside, slow, careful—like she was a storm I didn't want to scare into running again.

Like if I moved too fast, she'd shatter and disappear.

My eyes dragged over her—not to assess damage, but because I didn't know how to *not* look at her.

She was hunched against the wall, knees drawn in tight, one hand white-knuckling her coat like it was the only thing tethering her to the floor.

Her cheek was blotchy—either from the wind or crying.

Maybe both.

And her mouth was parted just enough to look like she'd been trying to speak, but the words got stuck somewhere deep.

She looked like a question I didn't know how to answer. And still, every cell in my body wanted to get down on my knees and be whatever she needed.

"Viv," I said.

Her name came out low. Raw. Something between a warning and a plea.

Not *come back*, not *don't run again*—just *I'm here.*

"Viv," I said again, softer this time. "It's me."

Like maybe she forgot.

Or maybe she didn't believe it was safe to believe that voice belonged to someone who wouldn't hurt her.

"Viv."

"It's not real," she whispered, the words breaking free like shards of glass. "The painting...the map...everything I believed in—it's all a lie. It's a *fake.*"

Her voice cracked on the last word, sharp and brittle like breaking glass, and in that instant, I knew—I had fucked up.

All the hours I'd spent chasing her through this godforsaken city, running down shadows and whispers, hoping to catch a glimpse of the woman I thought I was starting to reach...

Only to find out that everything I'd believed about her, about us, was built on a lie. The painting wasn't real.

The map, the mystery—her whole damn life had been spun from a forgery. I should have seen it coming.

Hell, maybe I did deep down. But I wanted to believe.

Wanted to believe that beneath all the walls, beneath the scars and the silence, there was something real to hold onto.

And now? Now I was standing in this abandoned studio with her, watching the fight drain out of her like spilled water, hearing the weight of a shattered dream in her voice.

I clenched my fists so tight my nails bit into my palms.

This wasn't how it was supposed to go. I wanted to be her anchor—not the reason she felt adrift.

I wanted to be the one who made her stop running, not the one who showed her there was nothing left to run *to*.

Her eyes met mine—drenched in pain, but also defiance.

She wasn't broken. Not yet.

But I could feel the cracks spreading, and if I didn't hold on, if I didn't say something that made sense, I'd lose her all over again.

"Vivianne," I breathed, raw and ragged.

"I'm here. I'm not going anywhere."

KIERAN

A FAKE.

She had a fake.

All this time.

Horrified was not the right word for how I felt chasing after the real deal and never having what I needed in the first place.

I'm such an idiot.

Why would Mamie even have the real one in the first place?

Probably not healthy but I felt like breaking something

I felt like snapping.

The moment I pulled her aside, the need for her consumed me. I couldn't resist the urge to have her closer. Closer.

Close enough to never let her leave.

To feel her against me.

Vivianne melted into me, her soft curves molding perfectly to my hard planes.

Stripping her out of her leggings with frenzied hands, the fabric falling to the floor in a forgotten heap.

"I want you. I do." She sank to her knees right there and took me in her mouth.

As I pressed into her, I swore under my breath, my eyes falling shut at the exquisite sensation.

I swore under my breath. My lashes shuttered, senses failing at the sensations of her. Her. Just her.

All over me.

Spinning her around, I bent her over, my hands gripping her hips.

"Oh fuck. There you go…" I groaned, sinking deeper into her.

Vivi squirmed adorably beneath me, her body struggling to accommodate my size.

The heat of her, without a condom, without anything between us, was driving me insane with need.

I had never felt a desperation like this before, a primal urge to claim her, to make her mine in every way possible.

A fake.

She had been chasing a goddamn fake.

All this time. Every sleepless night. Every risk. Every bargain made with ghosts and shadows…

It had all been for nothing.

Horrified wasn't the right word.

No, this was deeper. More bone-deep.

Like being gutted from the inside out and left to bleed in silence.

I pulled her aside—didn't even think—

I *needed* her.

Not just the way a man needs a woman, but in that holy, aching way you need air after drowning.

I needed to feel something *real*.

Her breath caught as I pressed her back against the wall. The hunger in me wasn't polished or patient—it was wild, cracked open by grief, by fury, by the unbearable weight of failing at everything that ever mattered.

Vivianne melted into me like she belonged there, like she *knew*.

Her soft curves against the hardness of me—the only softness in a brutal world.

I stripped her down with trembling hands, not from hesitation, but from need so sharp it bordered on agony.

Her leggings slid down her legs like silk unraveling, forgotten as they pooled at her feet.

I spun her around, palms searing into her hips, grounding myself in the heat of her skin.

Bent her forward—because I needed her to feel it, every bit of the ache coiled inside me.

"I want you," she whispered, voice wrecked and beautiful. "I do."

And then she sank to her knees, and for a moment—

I forgot.

I forgot the betrayal. The forgery. The loss.

Because it was just her.

Vivianne, mouth on me, and my hands tangled in her hair like a prayer I didn't know how to finish.

I groaned low in my throat, the sound involuntary—like something torn from the core of me.

My lashes shuttered. My spine bowed.

I could feel myself unraveling with every breath she stole, every motion that grounded me in *this*, in *now*—in her.

When I opened my eyes, the storm hadn't passed.

But she was there, kneeling in the middle of it.

And somehow, impossibly, I wasn't drowning alone anymore.

I wrapped my arms around her, holding her flush against my chest as I took her with a fierce intensity.

Her whimpers and moans spurred me on, each sound sending a bolt of pleasure straight to my core.

As I bottomed out, I held her tightly, savoring the feeling of being buried deep inside her, connected in the most intimate way possible.

Vivianne's inner walls clamped down on me desperately, her body responding to every thrust with a needy fervor.

"Kieran," she whispered breathlessly, her voice laced with desire. "Kieran, please."

With trembling hands, she guided my touch to her breasts, silently begging for more.

I groaned, my arousal heightening at her wanton plea. "Need more?" I asked, my voice thick with desire.

She nodded frantically, her body quivering beneath my touch.

I fucking loved this woman, her responsiveness, her unbridled passion.

My hands slipped under her shirt, seeking the soft mounds of her breasts.

As my fingers found her nipples, hard and straining against the fabric, I tugged on them simultaneously, reveling in the way her clenching intensified around my throbbing length.

"Oh fuck..." Vivi whimpered, her head falling back against my shoulder, her body surrendering to the pleasure I was giving her.

The familiar sensations of her impending release threatened to push me over the edge. "Are you coming, luv?" I groaned, marveling at how quickly she was unraveling in my arms.

Vivi nodded, her body trembling uncontrollably.

"Fuck, you're so fucking beautiful," I praised, my voice raw with emotion as I watched her lose herself.

With a deep, purposeful stroke, I surged back into her, burying myself to the hilt in her quivering heat.

Her hand flew to her mouth, desperately attempting to stifle the scream of pure bliss that threatened to tear from her throat

The sound was muffled, but the intensity of her pleasure was unmistakable.

Undeterred by her efforts to maintain silence, I set a relentless pace, my hips snapping against hers with a primal urgency.

I fucked her through the waves of her release, each powerful thrust drawing out the ecstasy that consumed her body.

I could feel her knees buckling, her body surrendering to the intense sensations that coursed through her.

But I refused to let her fall, my arms tightening around her waist like steel bands, holding her steady against my chest.

With unwavering determination, I continued to work my hips, driving into her with a need that bordered on obsession.

"Keep coming, luv."

22

VIVIANNE

It was late in the evening when we got home from dinner.

Kieran came out of the shower, dripping wet, with a towel around his waist. And nothing else. Amber eyes intense and laser-focused on me.

He's so pretty.

"Did you need me?"

Uhhhhh.

What did a girl say to that?

I swallowed and barely got a word out because he was on me in another second. He pounced. I was done.

Kieran reached between my legs and working his hand between my legs.

"No panties?"

"I r—tossed—erm—it's gone. They're gone."

A wide grin stretched his lips, canines flashing and eyes lighting up with mirth. It stretched into a wicked grin with nothing but dark intent.

And my insides turned a little watching him, but my thighs clenched together tightly unsure of what to do with him.

He didn't toss the towel to the side, instead he stepped closer. With me sitting down, I just watched him. I had been unsure for the last thirty minutes. What the hell did I even do?

"Want me?"

"Er—" *What did I even say?*

"Do you?" He tipped his head playfully. I thought he'd sit by me but instead he leaned into me and I felt myself taken down by all two-hundred-sixty pounds of man.

A light laugh left me nervous as he tore into my clothes gently.

"Watcha got there?"

A helpless giggle escaped me. *"Kieran—"*

"Do you—"

"Kieran—"

I felt his grin against my skin, my cheek, but I couldn't stop smiling.

I'm so sorry I was a total sneak. Coming into the bathroom.

He sealed his mouth over mine and I stopped thinking. I stopped thinking completely. Stopped functioning.

Loving this man is the best part of my day.

I didn't know who moved first, but he moved onto me, dropping his towel. And he was on me in another second.

My hands gripped his bicep, the muscles underneath bunching and tightening as he bore down on the bed. Pushing me down not-so-gently, but playfully and pressing until I felt him harder and hotter than iron on my thigh.

"Let me in."

I turned a bright shade of red. He didn't say much sometimes, but when he did he made it count. I just moved with him. Unable to even process what he was doing. Instead, I just didn't even think twice. I don't know what came over me.

I trusted him. I did.

But it was a little scary.

"Little thief, come here."

He pressed his nose into my cheek, his forehead against mine, nuzzling like a sun-warmed lion against my body. Comforting and strong, Kieran made it easier to breathe as I took him in and let him topple me into the bed. A delighted laugh left me.

"Why are you like this?"

"Why aren't you?"

"You're infuriating—"

121

"Am I?"

"Yes." But I was grinning ear to ear saying it.

Because I didn't know what to do. I just knew even if he took the lead I'd be okay even if it was terrifying even now.

After being with him all the time, every single damn day at the Primrose—I was still nervous because every single time with him, felt like the first time.

I was relearning how to love, learning how to let him love me, and slowly my goals were expanding to something other than what I originally had intended.

"Kieran."

"Hm?" He was on my neck in another second, his lips warmer than usual, and pressing hot kisses to my pulse. "Yeah?"

Nothing.

I couldn't think.

"Let me in."

I don't know who moved first or how he moved. I just knew I felt his hands at my pajama bottoms. Tugging. Lower. And a helpless noise leaving my lips.

I was holding on letting him take the lead.

A tug. A pull. Kieran's warm chest on mine, baring down on me not-so-gently.

Deep down, Kieran pressed and I liked that he knew. He *knew*.

I loved that he knew.

How to adjust. How to apply pressure. And I felt relief rushing through me as he pressed into me.

Even if I wasn't entirely ready, the idea of being with him alone made me soaking wet.

Kieran pressed and I winced a little.

Enough for him to stop and pause. A breath blew out of him gently on my pulse.

"I gotcha," he murmured lowering himself down more and more. "I gotcha. I gotcha."

He repeated it over and over again as he stayed right there.

"Better?"

I nodded my eyes having squeezed shut when I winced.

Thank God, he didn't move.

"Sorry," he whispered. "I gotcha." His head dipped and I closed my eyes as wet hot heat darted over my nipples. "*I gotcha.*"

I bit down on my lip a tiny bit as his mouth closed over as he pressed in. Every single time with him was like this.

I sobbed a little at the way he pressed, sliding in further with every tug.

Deeper. Further. *More.*

It ached enough for me to know how big he was, taking up all the space inside of me. But as he slowly bottomed out, I felt my eyes well.

As he wiped tears away and new ones formed. I wrapped my arms around his neck and tugged him lower.

For a man who didn't show the world he wanted to be held, he loved it.

I was expecting him to go faster, harder, rougher, but instead he moved in me languidly. Slow enough for me to know he was there. But enough for me to *feel* him.

It felt like I had never had sex before until him and when I clenched down on him, I came right then. It took me by surprise and a soft groan left him.

There you fucking go.

That's my girl.

One more. One more.

White hot sensation pooled low in my womb and I heard him dimly encouraging me through it which only made it more intense.

Noises left my lips and I couldn't think anymore.

When I calmed down he was brushing his lips over mine. He was still hard inside of me. I trembled.

"I need more." I panted as he began moving and I cried out sensitized from my earlier orgasm. "You're so sensitive. It drives me insane."

I sobbed as he began a pounding rhythm taking my mouth in his once more and I don't remember how many times I came just that I was a mess.

"Come for me." I couldn't anymore, I told him. "I know you want to let go." I did. I shook my head back and forth. No, no more.

"*One more,* just for *me,*" A noise left me as he pulled my hands down and held them down as his hips drove into my body.

Oh, I was so wet.

I was a ragged mess.

I'm never going to think he's cold ever again.

It shouldn't feel *this* good.

As I laid there by the last one I had, I was crying openly and he was over me groaning and moving with such purpose I felt like every stroke was lighting me up.

Mini orgasms stacked on top of each other.

And I couldn't do anything but lay there, surrendering completely—every barrier between us dissolving as he took my mouth in his.

I met him eagerly, breathless and aching, matching every claim he made with my own hunger, my own need.

Kieran's hands gripped me with fierce intent, driving his hips into mine with a desperate rhythm that swallowed everything whole.

His groan vibrated through me—raw, guttural—a sound that struck straight into my center, making me tremble like I was falling and flying all at once.

He filled every inch of me, consuming, claiming, making me feel seen and wanted in a way I'd never dared to hope.

He kept going, relentless and tender all at once, and I came and came, crashing over the edge again and again, until my body shook with the force of it.

I closed my eyes, lost in the storm of sensation—and when I finally opened them, the world had shifted.

I watched him. The man I thought was made of ice—cold and untouchable—was raw and curious, vulnerable in ways he rarely showed.

He tilted his head like a wolf sizing me up, fierce and beautiful, his eyes searching mine for something deeper than desire.

"I love you," I whispered, my voice breaking.

And for a moment everything stopped for me.

I couldn't breathe through my own emotions.

"I love you."

I pressed our foreheads together, the heat of him grounding me, making me brave enough to say it again—

"I love you, I love you, I—"

23

VIVIANNE

I woke up warmer than I'd ever been.

And I needed heat. I was so warm. I stirred in bed rolling onto my stomach.

I squeaked when the warmth rolled on top of me.

Over the last few days Kieran O'Hara had gotten under my skin. I was falling for this guy. His curling hair at the ends, his smile, sharper-canines. Amber eyes. Easy laughter. And his warmth. I was falling for him more than I could accept.

And so I welcomed it. I did.

I could enjoy it even temporarily right?

Erik did.

He was in a relationship with the girl he'd met in school. And now I was the odd-ball out. Always invisible. Always hustling. And Kieran too.

Turns out I had a lot in common with him.

And I hadn't expected that. Hadn't expected him to sneak up on me. Hadn't expected him to be there for me the way he had. Hadn't expected him to be with me and take care of me. And get me bagels. Get me food. Take care of me. Put on my socks. Love me.

Love me.

That was a foreign concept. That wasn't something I was ever used to. The butterflies in my stomach were very much real and very much upset whenever his warmth went away.

His hugs. His laughter. And his teasing.

That wasn't something I ever thought I deserved but when Kieran was around me—I was like a woman in a drought. Looking for an oasis. Constantly.

I had money.

He had time.

And it was…it felt perfect. Perfect.

And I was waiting for the glass to shatter beneath my Mahnolo's knowing full well it wasn't healthy. No. But it was all I knew.

A masculine chuckle low and deep behind me made me clench as he opened my legs and I had a moment to process what was happening—and then I moaned into the pillows as he entered me.

Oh God, the entire night came crashing back over me.

He was huge and I panted taking him deep, as he bottomed out sinking so deep a groan left both of us.

"You're so wet. Did you dream about me?"

I had dreamt nothing. Blissfully it was so dark and sweet.

"You blacked out after your orgasms. I lost count of which number you were on."

Me too. I heard him groaning as he moved, grinding and then finally settling deep. I panted.

"I love the way you say my name." His soft confessions would undo me any day. "Like it's the best thing in the world—"

"You are." It left my throat hoarse from screaming and in the morning. *"You are mine."*

"Yeah," he rasped. "I am." And he moved.

I screamed into the pillows at the position. Above me he groaned. It was so deep. So *deep* like this.

"Yeah, it is." I was shaking to have said it out loud but he didn't care, as he groaned and moved.

I screamed with every thrust and how deep he was. "Arch your back just a little."

I was afraid of what—I shrieked louder than the other times as I did. And his chuckle was dark. *"Good girl."*

And then in that position he began to drill into me.

127

"You're so sensitive after your first orgasm, come on, pretty baby, let me have it."

I came with the second thrust. A strangled scream left me, I was *sensitive.*

Behind me he let out a low laugh, and I was so embarrassed and wholly his. I let go.

I couldn't think, only feel, white hot pleasure blossomed and I gasped and cried. Sobbed his name. *Only him.*

I was *coming*—and then he groaned over me moving and I couldn't think anymore.

Everything was centered in that spot. That place where he pounded into me whispering the filthiest things in my ear.

"Such a good girl, aren't you? Letting me destroy that little pussy first thing in the morning. Gonna start and end my days in your heat. You are mine. You'll come only for me. Only on my cock."

Yesyesyes. I was screaming, disjointed and laying there getting absolutely pummeled.

Somewhere his fingers found mine and I latched on as he locked them over my head. His thrusts grew rougher with the contact, and I screamed as I came in with the force. It was so sweet, so—

"*Right there?*" He came down harder and an animal noise left my lips as he repeatedly slammed in.

He groaned as he finally came and I couldn't keep it in. I began to cry as I came.

Tears spilled down my cheeks and I let out a noise, between a whimper and a mewl. He settled over me and I sobbed into the bed.

"Baby?" His voice changed and I reached back gripping his head close to mine as he moved his lips over my ear, my cheek.

Dating a man with the exterior of a Rottweiler was not on my bingo card.

No.

I wasn't used to dating. Let alone dating a man like him.

But I lit up from the inside out when he was inside of me. I couldn't think straight and Kieran would lick my lips like some hungry wolf and bite down with a wicked smile.

"That's the point—"

I just kissed him quiet.

Kieran moved inside of me like he had a score to settle with my body. I couldn't think.

I could only feel. I could only love him.

In whatever variation of love I saw fit. I held his face as he settled in and clenched down on him.

He was so big, he took up every inch of space inside of me until I couldn't breathe unless he lifted up on his elbows.

Amber eyes met mine with a tender softness I hadn't expected from him as he brushed my hair back.

"Better?"

"Mhm."

I could do this all day. Every day.

The thought crept into my mind with the grace of avalanche.

It was slow to build and as it did, it spiraled out, blossoming into a bud and then taking root in my chest.

I could fall in love with Kieran if I'm not careful.

"You are more than enough," he murmured watching me. "Everything you are is more than enough for me."

I stilled. Unmoving. Unblinking.

What?

I couldn't form words or coherent thoughts.

I don't know how to love without you.

The thought crept into my mind again. And again as he sank deeper and deeper. Kieran settled over me and the deeper he went the less uncomfortable it became. But he took up all the space around me adjusting the comforter.

I thought he might kiss me as I rocked my hips up urging him to move. Urging him to do anything but watch me. Make me vulnerable.

And I felt my throat tighten, eyes welling with unfamiliar emotion.

"Are you good? I can feel your thighs shaking."

"Sorry—"

"Don't be—"

"No—"

"I can do this—"

What?

And then he sank down fully and held deep.

"You'll make love to me?"

Where did that come from?

It left my lips before I could even stop it.

"Yeah," he puffed out a hot breath over my cheek. "I will. Hang tight. I'm trying not to lose it."

He blinked slowly, tipping his head. "I would give you anything you want. Everything you need. Just say the word."

"I want you." I wanted him like I needed to breathe. "Just you."

Kieran was a force of nature.

And when he was playful he was at his worst.

By the time he started moving I was a wreck. And he kept going. It was slow and tender and steady and I died a little.

Coming down from my second orgasm, I was so sensitive, I felt little micro-shocks running through me.

I gasped for him to speed up, and with how hard I shook, he dropped his body on me. I couldn't even look into his eyes, and he nudged his arm under my neck bringing me to him.

He slowed down so much I sighed calming down.

Amber eyes meeting mine filled with heat and love flushing his body against mine.

I felt one with him in so many ways right then. I whimpered a little, squeezing my eyes shut, taking him deeper. Easier.

"I *know*..." he crooned in that voice of his. "Poor baby...are you tired?"

No. I could love him forever. Hold him to me like this. Keep him in my heart.

I opened my eyes to see his watching me with soft love in them, a little tease. He was dangerous when he was happy.

"No? No more?" He was *dangerous*. "I think you have one more...just for me." Dangerous. He was dangerous when he was playful.

I sobbed into his lips as I kissed him, his body picking up inside of me. Why did he have this much energy? He smiled against my lips. "Just one more..."

I'm in bed with the devil.

His eyes never left as he began pounded into me, his pants over my lips and I loved it. I clung to him as he hit deep, somewhere so sweet, I cried out.

Soft cries left me then as he hit that spot unrelentingly. There was nothing I could keep from him. No part of me left to hide.

I sobbed into his mouth. *"Kieran."*

"Right there...I *know*...Don't fight it...give it over to me..." I could feel it forming quicker than the hours.

Every single time he did this, I came faster and faster, and he loved it. His low lidded amber eyes watched me as he moved, taking his lower lip into his mouth and I was crying now.

"Little thief. You're going to come again, aren't you?" I was, but he knew that. He knew my body better than me sometimes. "Let me have it, don't look away, eyes on me."

I blinked my tears as I met them and my orgasm rocked through me, a strangled noise leaving me, as he gasped never leaving me. Holding me steady.

Holding his gaze. *"Kieran."*

A soft smile stretched his lips as I came. "You are so beautiful."

I sobbed with pleasure as he pounded me through it, kissing me working me through it until I was screaming, begging, tearing my eyes away as he held fast to me.

"Don't fight it—" he whispered his voice dark in my ear. "Don't fight me...let go, let me have it...*that's so good. Good girl....Keep going. I know you have more...*"

～

WHEN I WOKE UP I MADE A NOISE.

I must've made something because I felt myself pulled up to a hard chest and Kieran's dark growls.

Come on, baby, just a little—I felt him pressing something to my lips. I whimpered, unsure of how I felt. Like *out of it.*

"I'm not going to let you drop, okay? I got you. Come on. Just a little more for me," I sipped obediently, aware Kieran had fucked me into this state. And he was trying to feed me.

"Just a little more."

Don't fight it. Don't fight it...

Let go.

No more? Yes, one more one more come on pretty baby....

I was a mess. How many orgasms I'd I have?

Kieran called me sensitized and I was.

Very.

And whenever I came to, in his arms cuddled close and he tried to always get me to drink something first before trying to feed me.

I laid there taking in his scent, the feel of my body against his hard lines, the way it rose and fell and I woke up to him every morning.

Kieran cleaned me up and took care of me. But I also did that for him.

Once I tied him up while he was asleep one day he was tired. I woke him up tied to the bed handcuffed and I slowly went down on him, slowly, and it drove him crazy.

I kissed all over him and down his body loving his face, loving him. Everywhere.

When I finally got to his cock and took him, he'd groaned long and low. His hips automatically working into my mouth, and I loved it.

I had been afraid to let him out at the way he had watched me low lidded and hungry.

He was going to—I screamed as he lunged and threw me down, the first thrust making me cry out and every one after that driving me mad he was so turned on he could do nothing but fuck —and for me to take

I screamed his name as I came and he pumped harder.

"You're going to kill me."

I felt his lips move over my back. "Don't say that, I intend to keep you."

24

VIVIANNE

We ended up on the hotel room floor, the discarded takeout containers scattered around us like some makeshift midnight picnic—messy, imperfect, and completely ours.

The city lights flickered beyond the windows, a distant, sparkling world full of noise and chaos.

But all I could focus on was the man sitting across from me—the one who, against all odds, had managed to pull me out of the darkness and make me feel something close to human again.

He wasn't just a stranger with secrets or a shadow lurking in the background. He was something real. Something solid.

Someone who felt just as awful as I did all the time.

Someone who his family forgot about.

Someone who never was chosen by anybody.

Choose me.

Just choose me.

But I couldn't say those things.

Kieran never felt accepted or loved by anybody.

And neither had I.

I saw my Mamie slipping away.

He saw his mother slipping away.

His father abused him.

I never had mine.

My life was about my brother. His life was about his.

Neither one of us had anyone to focus on us.

And I was an idiot for even thinking we were perfect sometimes because I didn't know how effortless it was for the thought to cross my mind.

His brothers were always working around the clock to ensure his families success. I was doing the same. But just differently.

I saw Kieran as someone worth—seeing.

More than just…himself. More than…a problem.

But sometimes I wondered if he saw me as a problem. Because thats all I had ever been. A problem for everyone. So I became my own solution.

And I realized the more I talked to Kieran the more I realized the values we learned were the same.

We didn't cry.

We didn't scream.

We didn't shout.

We didn't ask why.

We saw a problem.

And we fixed it.

The end.

The world that had overlooked me and Kieran wouldn't overlook me ever again. Except, I wasn't sure if I ever wanted the world to see me. Maybe Kieran did. Maybe he dreamed one day the world would recognize him. See him as more than just a man.

But me?

I wanted to fly under the radar. Forever.

I knew I existed.

But I couldn't live like him.

Surrounded by bodyguards. Everyone knew his name.

Nobody knew mine.

That's the way I preferred it.

Nobody could know me.

And I didn't know how to tell Kieran I didn't know how to be a part of his world. I wasn't chasing visibility.

I was chasing peace.

~

"How do you make your money when you don't kill people?" I asked, my voice quiet but edged with curiosity, as if testing the boundaries of this fragile connection.

Kieran's grin spread slow and wide, a spark lighting up his eyes like I'd just cracked some private joke between us. It was the kind of smile that made you forget the weight of the world, even if just for a moment.

In that smile, I saw a glimpse of the man beneath the armor—the man who could still laugh, still play, still hope.

And maybe, just maybe, I was starting to fall for him.

Not because I trusted easily, or because I believed life was suddenly going to be simple. But because with him, I remembered what it felt like to breathe without holding my breath.

For the first time in a long time, I didn't want to run.

I wanted to stay.

Right there.

With him.

It transformed his whole face, softening the hard edges I'd grown used to.

"Well, a few years ago, my brother and his friend figured out an extensive long-term plan. Forty years worth." He leaned back against the couch, soda in hand, looking more relaxed than I'd ever seen him. "Something to get us out of the shit show we were in."

"What kind of plan?"

"Aidan took all these abandoned properties we were using for..." he smirked, leaving the activities unnamed. "Kieran told him to turn them legitimate. Convert everything to apartments. Now real estate's our biggest portfolio."

The casual way he discussed converting criminal enterprises into legitimate business should have scared me.

Instead, I found myself fascinated by how his mind worked.

"You own all the shops? And bars?"

"Surprised?"

"Yeah, I wasn't expecting that. Figured it'd be more..." I waved my chopsticks vaguely. "Stereotypical mob stuff."

"We diversified. The bars belong to different shell companies, the properties are managed by separate entities. Everything's connected but separate."

I studied him in the dim light, this man who'd transformed his family's criminal empire into something sustainable. Who looked at broken things and saw potential. Who looked at me and saw...what exactly?

"What?" he asked, catching my stare.

"Nothing. Just trying to figure you out."

His smile turned softer. "How's that going?"

"You're nothing like I expected," I admitted, surprising myself with my honesty.

The city lights painted shadows across his face as he considered this. "Good different or bad different?"

I took another bite of food to avoid answering immediately. Because the truth was, O'Hara was becoming dangerously different in all the ways that mattered.

"Surprised?" He asked, looking amused at my reaction to their business empire.

"Yeah, I wasn't expecting that."

He gestured toward the restaurant bags between us. "Nisha owns this place. Well, technically Killian does, but it was a gift for her." The way his face softened when he mentioned his sister-in-law spoke volumes. "And through Titan we're private contractors, plus I run the Blue Cross Initiative—"

"The one that rehabilitates felons with actual skills?" I sat up straighter, intrigued.

"Yup."

"What the—"

"Gabriel's idea. Builds loyalty." He shifted, getting more comfortable. "Most of them end up working for us or Titan. Though Reed thinks they're a headache."

"I met Reed in Chicago," I offered, watching him pick through his food.

"Yeah, he hates leaving Alisha and Rhys behind," Kieran said, his chopsticks pausing. "But he likes staying involved. Gives us an edge."

"How much do you actually own?" I found myself genuinely curious, drawing my knees up to my chest.

"Most of Chicago." He started explaining the territory, the revitalization projects, the network of businesses.

"You did all that?"

He shrugged, humble in a way that surprised me. "Not me. Reed handles real estate with his team. You haven't met Nathan Wyatt but he's crucial too." He broke down the structure—O'Haras owning bars, Devereaux's holding properties, Wyatt handling liquor, Teaser's providing entertainment.

Watching him explain his world, comfortable and open in a way I'd never seen, I realized how easily I could get used to this. To him. To nights spent on hotel floors, sharing food and secrets like we were normal people.

That thought should have terrified me more than it did.

A comfortable silence had settled between us before spoke again, his voice softer than usual.

"Can I ask you something? About when you were working?"

I stiffened slightly, but the way he asked—careful, respectful— made me nod.

For the first time in years, I felt like a normal girl. No masks, no acts, no calculated moves.

Just me, sitting here with a man who'd somehow seen past all my carefully constructed walls. Kieran wasn't using me. Didn't need anything from me. The realization was both freeing and terrifying.

Deep down, I had to admit I liked him. Really liked him.

The thought sent conflicting emotions racing through me.

Desire. Self-preservation.

I don't know who moved first. Maybe I leaned in, drawn by the warmth in his amber eyes.

Maybe he closed the distance, finally giving in to whatever had been building between us. All I know is one moment we were talking, and the next his mouth was on mine.

The kiss was nothing like the calculated ones I'd given in the past to people.

This was heat and hunger. Something dangerously close to something tender.

His hands tangled in my hair like he'd been dying to touch me for weeks, and maybe he had. I gripped his shirt, pulling him closer as the kiss deepened.

For once, I wasn't thinking about escape routes or angles or what I could gain. I was just feeling—his warmth, his touch, the way he held me like I was something precious instead of broken.

In that moment, I wasn't his prisoner, and he wasn't my captor. We were just two people finding something real in a world built on pretense.

"We shouldn't," he breathed against my neck, his voice low, almost a warning—but his hands were already sliding beneath the jacket I wore, warm and familiar against my skin.

"You're sore."

"Probably not," I whispered, pulling him closer without hesitation, wrapping one leg around his hip. I could feel the solid, steady strength beneath my touch, the controlled power he always held like a secret weapon.

"Want to stop?"

His answer was a quiet, fierce lift, and suddenly I was in his arms, carried with a precision that was all muscle and intention.

The world narrowed to the sound of our breaths, the heat of his body pressed against mine as he moved toward the bed.

I didn't wait. I pulled him down with me, craving the weight of him, needing to feel him break free of the careful control he kept locked inside.

"Vivianne," he said, his voice rough and heavy, pulling back just enough for me to see the fire burning in his amber eyes—not just desire, but something raw and deeper.

"If we do this..."

I knew.

I knew exactly what he meant.

I knew who he was.

Even if it felt like I didn't know who *I* was anymore.

"And that doesn't scare you?"

It did.

It terrified me.

No more games.

No more masks.

No more pretending.

This was us—real, raw, unguarded.

Undamaged.

Beneath the twilight skyline, the city lights casting long shadows that danced across our skin, I found something I hadn't dared hope for—healing.

In him.

For the first time in a long time, I wasn't calculating angles or plotting escapes.

For once, I was just feeling—his hands tangled in my hair, his mouth tracing the curves of my skin, the way he touched me like I wasn't just a little thief or a broken girl.

Like I was something precious.

Something worth fighting for.

Something more.

KIERAN

VIVIANNE SMELLED LIKE PEACH RINGS.

I inhaled the taste of tangy sugar on her tongue. Electric. Wild. That was one way of describing her.

She giggled into my kisses. And I didn't know I'd find it endearing.

I loved making *love* to her.

Before Vivianne I was fucking around. I was fucking with everything I could.

But now?

I *liked* Vivianne. I liked her more than I could admit.

She wasn't a stranger to me with secrets. A problem. She wasn't a problem.

She was striving. Always striving. Always trying. Always fighting. She was real.

She was just like me.

Bold.

Beautiful.

Wildly wonderful.

She was real.

So fucking real.

Something solid.

Someone who felt the way I did.

Someone who the world forgot about.

Choose me.

Just choose me.

But I couldn't say those things.

She had never felt accepted or loved by anybody. And neither had I. I had struggled with my relationship with my brothers, my parents that weren't around, my sister-in-laws—and everyone else around me doubting me.

Did I know I was keeping secrets from her?

I didn't feel like an idiot for even thinking we were perfect.

Sometimes I didn't know how effortless it would feel like to be around a woman.

I had felt overlooked in many ways and I didn't know how to tell her I knew about her history as a call-girl. I knew what she did for a living. I knew what she didn't do. And I knew all the down-sides to being in a relationship with her.

Or without her.

I wasn't sure if I ever wanted to be like Aidan or Killian. Nor would I ever be. But it didn't matter.

Not with her and I couldn't put my finger on it.

Because I was pretending to be someone I wasn't?

I became someone I was. And by stopping being the person I thought I was I became someone new-er. New-ish. With her.

I always thought I would be like Aidan. Rougher or tougher on the outside but not the inside.

Or like Killian with his picture perfect life with Nisha.

Neither one of my brothers were cold, abusive, or negligent.

No. The opposite. Neither one had taken after my parents. And neither had I.

But I didn't want to be...Aidan or Killian. I wanted to be myself.

But me?

I didn't want to fly under the radar. Forever.

I knew I existed. I wanted people to know I existed.

But I couldn't live like Vivianne.

Not surrounded by aid. Nobody knew if she lived or died.

That's the way I preferred it.

And I didn't know how to tell Vivianne I didn't know how to be a part of her world without introducing her to mine.

I wasn't chasing her.

I was chasing everything about her.

Inhaling peach rings whenever I kissed her, sucking on her tongue. I couldn't get her taste out of my mouth.

Faint echoes of it on the back of my throat. I could kiss her for hours.

It was like she had melted into my very being, the impression of her permanently infused into my taste buds. I was marked by her. And in turn, I returned it.

I moved as she came apart and I groaned, feeling the moment she lost it, clamping down on me.

"Eyes on me, baby."

Keep those eyes on me, beautiful. "That's it...stay with me."

I moved stroking her, feeling her pulsing, and it took everything to stay on her, once her eyes met mine though? It took everything not to come with her.

But I loved watching her come apart. I watched her lose focus, eyes low lidded and *so fucking pretty*, as I pumped, biting down on her lip, as tears streamed down her cheeks.

And she'd never looked more beautiful. She came harder when she kept her eyes on me.

There was nothing like her.

I kept my arm behind her neck as I slowed my thrusts driving deep and holding.

Vivianne gasped and sobbed my name against my lips. Pleading. Begging.

"I know..." I never looked away knowing it took her effort as her mouth turned down like she was in pain, struggling to keep her eyes. A shaky exhale left her.

I was licking her lips, feeling like I was feeding off her orgasms. "You're so sensitive, for me, aren't you?"

I loved the way she nodded, her hand coming up to hold my cheek, and I smiled into it.

Keeping my eyes on hers, I confessed. "Nothing will come close to you, nobody has ever been *you*. You are mine. Every part of you. Your body, heart, soul, it will always…be mine."

I smiled as her tears streamed harder when I ground deeper.

I closed my eyes, sighing at the sound of that soft accent.

Even like this she filled me with that heat. The one that warmed my soul. This woman would hold my soul in hers. I had never loved anyone the way I loved her.

"Vivianne," I whispered against her lips. "I'm just getting started with you tonight," I smiled at the sound of her whimper. "I love how you come for me. Just me, baby. Isn't that right?" I wanted to grin at the feel of her clenching harder and harder.

The moment I moved my hips back she closed her eyes, her face telling me she was already sensitized. I did smile.

How did I get you?

"You are so perfect for me."

This time I *snapped* my hips back in, my lips at her pulse fluttering knowing she loved that spot, the one spot on her neck that I knew made her scream.

I groaned feeling her around me. It took everything not to come with her but I focused on her.

Vivianne.

My woman.

"I can feel that…come on, baby," I thrust in, loving the way she squealed. "Just one more for me…" I knew she was close already.

A whimper left her. A sob. *Fuck*, I loved those noises.

I knew my girl, I lifted my head to take her eyes. "You need my eyes?" She nodded. "Yeah? It's better, *isn't* it?"

She nodded desperately.

Focus on me, Vivianne.

I worked with her relentlessly, loving how she gasped against my lips, I never looked away.

"That's it, come on baby…Good girl."

I groaned, forcing myself to stay focused on her pleasure as she stiffened, her mouth opening, as she shook and clamped down on me.

I didn't stop pounding that little spot that drove her insane, loving how wet she grew, the sound of me working in her making her flush.

She sobbed my name over and over and I didn't stop. I'd never stop.

I saw the moment it was too much and her eyes fluttered rolling back and that drove me over my edge.

I gripped the headboard with my free hand using it as leverage to give.

"I know," I crooned, working in her like an animal then taking my pleasure, loving the continuous noise that came from fucking her.

Her frantic screams increased as she shook her head desperately.

"Kieran, *too much—*"

I felt a wicked grin form on my lips as I fucked deep.

"Don't fight it…. just let me have it….." I slammed in closing my eyes at the feel of how completely soaked she was.

Over and over again.

It was so fucking good. I groaned as she came on the heels of her previous orgasm sobbing wildly. I love this woman. T

his time I buried deep and gave myself over. Ohhhh fuck. Every sane thought left my brain as I slowed pumping her full. I was panting, kissing every bit of her I could put my mouth on.

"You did such a good job, baby…*baby?*"

And then my lips stretched into a low laugh.

She passed out.

I LET HER REST WHILE I CLEANED HER UP, I LOVED HOW SHY SHE GOT.

I liked pushing her past her limits, and I loved the love in her eyes as she crested and let me.

Every single time. Nothing would be her. Nobody would ever compare.

I took her in my arms not remembering if I ever cuddled anyone close.

She settled limp and pliant and I tucked her into my chest. Her hair spilled over the sheets, my pillows, and her scent was all over me.

My lips against her temple felt right as she didn't move. Sweet girl.

For all the confidence she portrayed, I loved seeing the way I could make her blush.

My fingers tangling in her hair, I made promises against her skin.

Take care of you.

Keep you safe.

I attributed it to her razor-sharp wit, the way she effortlessly challenged me, and I reveled in it.

Her bold attitude, her brilliant mind, she was better than me in every way she could be—I was utterly *captivated*.

Stunningly gorgeous, she was a force of nature, yet possessed a serene elegance.

Her melodic accent flowed through the depths of my being, permeating the icy caverns of my soul, thawing and transforming everything in its wake.

With her, I wanted the world. To become the absolute best version of myself. For her.

Vivianne was the singular facet of my existence that didn't require any machinations.

No intricate strategies, no carefully orchestrated deceptions. Honesty flowed effortlessly with her.

I treated her with the utmost respect and care, for she was worthy of nothing less. I slept on her heart.

Letting her go was never a thought I wanted to consider. She had infiltrated the very essence of my being, and I wanted for her to remain there.

From the hospital bed to here, I didn't want to let her go. She got under my skin, and I wanted her to stay there forever.

I wanted to keep her safe. Because she made me feel safe.

She is my home.

Her heart is my life.

I didn't even want to consider a world where I didn't wake up to her.

"Vivianne," I whispered. "Wake up."

I needed to make sure she had something in her otherwise she'd feel like shit.

"Come on, baby. I know you're tired, that's it, come here."

I memorized every curve on her body, every brush of her, the way she stirred.

I knew her.

I felt her in my soul. She was mine.

I pounded her back down into the bed and kept going.

"Come for me," she panted. "Please come inside me."

I growled brutally pounding into her loving her screams as she realized I did in fact have stamina for days and I held back with her a lot.

I grabbed the headboard and pounded in and out of her body loving the way she had shaken begging me to stop then.

26

KIERAN

I woke to cold sheets where Vivianne should have been.

My eyes snapped open, immediately scanning the room—empty bed, silent bathroom, her clothes from last night still scattered across the floor.

The anklet lay discarded by the couch, its light permanently dark.

Fuck.

Something twisted in my chest, sharp and slow—like grief hadn't quite figured out how to crawl out of me yet.

I sat up, heart thudding in the quiet, mind already racing ahead.

Of course she was gone. This was what she'd been waiting for—a moment of weakness, a chance to run.

There was no reason for her to stay, no reason for last night to have meant anything beyond escape. Because there was no painting anymore.

No leverage.

Fuck, I hated thinking like that. That was my...woman. I was just warming up to that idea and then some. I liked the girl.

Nothing left but a night neither of us could take back, and a silence that now echoed louder than her laughter ever had.

I leaned back against the headboard, trying to ignore how

hollow my chest felt. Stupid. Fucking stupid to let my guard down, to think—The hotel room door eased open.

And there she was.

Vivianne.

Carrying a paper bag and two coffee cups like she hadn't just gutted me.

Like she hadn't just left a Kieran-shaped hole in the goddamn mattress.

Her hair was a mess—my mess.

She wore nothing but my shirt from last night, sleeves pushed up, collar slipping off one shoulder.

She froze when she saw me sitting up, and for the first time in what felt like *forever*, she looked unsure.

Not calculating.

Not guarded.

Just…caught.

A soft, guilty flush crept up her neck.

"I got bagels?" she offered, voice light, like we were normal. Like this was normal.

Relief hit me so hard it felt like impact.

A punch to the gut. A breath I hadn't realized I was holding until she stepped back into it.

"You came back," I said, and it came out lower than I meant. Rougher.

Vivianne shrugged one shoulder like it was no big deal, but the tremble in her fingers as she set the breakfast down gave her away.

"Yeah, well…" She crawled back into bed, toes cold against my legs, the scent of street air and sugar clinging to her skin. "Turns out I'm pretty chill when I'm not trying to rob you."

I didn't laugh. Couldn't.

I just pulled her into me, burying my face in her hair—partly to breathe her in, mostly so she wouldn't see what was on my face.

Because I couldn't say it yet.

Couldn't tell her what it meant.

That she didn't run.

That she came back.

She could've vanished.

Could've taken the out.

But instead, she brought me coffee.

She chose *this*.

"Your coffee's getting cold," she whispered against my chest, voice softer now, like the moment was too fragile to speak above a hush.

"Don't care."

I held her tighter, every inch of me grounding against her body like I could make this real, make it last.

And when she smiled into my skin, I felt it—not just on my chest, but somewhere deep.

Somewhere I hadn't let anyone touch in a long, long time.

"Don't laugh," she said, pulling open the fridge. "I don't know how to cook. Like, at all. My brother does, but I mostly just lived on toast and hustle."

I leaned on the counter, sipping my coffee and trying not to smile. "I'm not laughing."

She eyed me over her shoulder. "You're definitely judging."

"Only a little." I gestured to the fridge. "Alright, show me what you've got."

She stepped aside like she was bracing for impact. Inside: a sad jar of mustard, a half-used lemon, two energy drinks, and what might have been cheese in a past life.

"I was gonna go shopping," she mumbled.

"Sure." I tried not to grin. "For...batteries and expired dairy?"

She stuck out her tongue and reached for a spoon. "Okay, *chef*, what would you make with this gourmet spread?"

Because this wasn't survival. This wasn't sex or strategy or secrets.

This was what people did when they *chose* each other.

27

KIERAN

Vivianne was practically vibrating as we climbed the stairs to Erik's apartment. Not just nerves—*protective* nerves.

The kind that came from years of holding the world on her shoulders.

It was a modern building. Good security. Clean lines, polished entry, probably a doorman downstairs trained to stay out of trouble.

Definitely a step up from anywhere either of us had grown up.

I figured Chicago Titan had stepped in—kept an eye on the kid from a distance.

But nothing prepared me for the actual moment.

The door opened, and there he was. Erik.

Tall, lanky, awkward in the way only med students and genius-level kids could be. Messy hair, bright eyes, an easy grin that lit up his whole face—until he saw me.

Then he froze.

"You're...O'Hara?" He blinked between me and Vivianne, his brain clearly trying to catch up. Why was *his* sister standing next to *Chicago's* most notorious crime boss?

I lifted my hands slightly, voice calm. "I'm a friend of your sister's."

That seemed to settle him—somewhat. But the real shift came from Vivianne.

She exhaled. Shoulders lowering. Eyes scanning him like she had to see it for herself. That he was okay. Safe.

And he was. You could feel it in the space—there was no tension here, no survival clawing at the edges.

Just textbooks scattered across counters, half-drunk coffee cups breeding in corners, and a kind of neatness that felt inherited.

Their grandmother's touch lingered in the way the throw pillows were arranged. The scent of lemon cleaner clinging to the air.

They had made it here. Somehow.

Over breakfast—takeout bagels, cheap coffee, Erik rattling off med school horror stories—I watched them. Watched *her*, really.

Vivianne leaned in, laughed with her whole face, corrected his stories mid-sentence. She softened in a way I didn't see often.

No mask. No edge.

And Erik…he looked at her like she was his whole world.

I already had a file on him, of course. I knew his grades, his part-time jobs, the loan Titan quietly paid off behind the scenes.

But now I *knew* him.

It wasn't until I ducked into the bathroom that I saw it.

An enormous comic book poster dominated one wall.

Something vintage—washed out reds and bold lines, a classic cover from a graphic novel series I'd seen before.

Except something about it was…off.

I stepped closer.

The corner was peeling. Just slightly. Not enough for most people to notice. But I wasn't most people.

There was another layer underneath. A texture too rich for cheap ink and paper.

And instinct kicked in.

I snapped a photo and texted Liam with a quick note.

Because if what I thought was true—Erik Valentine wasn't just a med student.

He was the reason Vivianne never stopped running.

G, is he working with Greenie?

He's got a replica of the map on the two paintings in his dorm room

Reina never said a word

About that—we might have a problem with that

Nash Group found the treasure already

It's in the bottom of the gold pool Malcolm Nash had put in

Now I was stumped.

What?

The bottom of the fucking compound had buried fucking treasure

I'm in Cape Verde right now

I shit you not

What?

Pics or it didn't happen

Its been three weeks since you've been shacked up with her

She doesn't know you told us the painting was fake and her brother has no fucking clue we're spying on them

Or we're fucking him over

Reina makes sure he goes to school online only so he doesn't interact with his friends anymore

And the money?

We can put a cut into her bank account but everything is Nash Groups

As cold as it is?

It belongs to Talia and Natasha but if she wants a cut, Talia doesn't want or need it

Drew doesn't give a shit

Natasha's too pregnant to complain

Fuck

"How the fuck am I supposed to tell Viv this shit?"

Her eyes sparkled, lighter somehow—less guarded—as she settled into the small apartment that still held traces of their grandmother's careful touch.

It was a moment of peace, fragile and bright.

But the calm shattered the second I spoke.

"What?" she asked, her voice already sharp—like she *knew* I was hiding something.

I turned to her, jaw tight. "I was protecting you—"

"Bullshit." The word cracked through the air like a slap. "You weren't protecting me, Kieran. You were *controlling* me. Just like everyone else."

"The compound isn't safe," I said, setting my glass down harder than I meant to. "Nash Group has security that would—"

"That's *not your choice to make!*" she shouted, her hands trembling at her sides. Her whole body was wound tight, color flushing high on her cheeks, voice raw with something that sounded like grief.

"That painting is my *family's* legacy. My grandmother—"

"Would want you alive!" I shot back. "You think I don't understand what it means to you? Why do you think I sent Titan instead of letting you walk into a fucking death trap?"

Her eyes shone, furious and wounded. "Because you don't trust me."

"No." My voice dropped, thick and breaking. "Because I can't lose you."

Silence.

The kind that echoed louder than any scream.

"You're so hellbent on throwing yourself into the fire for this—

this *ghost*! Like dying for it will make any of it hurt less! Like it'll bring her back. But it won't."

Her lip trembled. She looked like she wanted to hit me. Or cry. Or both.

"You don't need the money. I took care of Erik. I took care of *you*—"

"I didn't ask you to!" she choked out, voice cracking. "I didn't ask you to fix my life, Kieran. I asked you to *see* me."

And that's when I realized—

She thought I only wanted to save her.

But all I wanted was *her*. Mess and all.

"I don't fucking want your money!"

"Because you're spoiled already!"

She froze as I said it. I couldn't stop. "You're *spoiled*. You think everything in life owes you something. Life owes you nothing. It owes you nothing! I'm sorry your grandmother died. I'm sorry for what that man did to you! I have done every single thing in my fucking power to fix it for you! I am trying."

I felt my heart cracking in places I didn't know could break. "I am sorry for your life and your suffering. I am giving you ways to not suffer anymore—"

"By sticking an anklet on me—"

"It's the only way you won't run!" I yelled, voice cracking under the weight of everything I'd been holding in. "You're too damn fucking afraid of everyone else. You don't stick around. Even with Erik—you keep him at arm's length like he's some stranger. I have Lawless stalking him, making sure the kid's got friends, making sure he's *okay!*"

She paled at my words, taking a step back like I'd punched her in the gut.

Because she didn't know.

She didn't know I'd been watching over *her* brother, too—trying to give him the kind of support she was too scared to fully give.

"Everyone's tried to kill me and my brothers," I said, the memories cutting through my chest like a blade. "My mother hated me from the day I was born—because my father raped her. You want to know why? Because she had an affair and had Killian. He's my half-brother. He doesn't even know."

I swallowed hard. "My father beat Killian like a dog growing up...because of his eyes."

I ran my hands through my hair, the frustration boiling over. "You want to know what changed? Killian found Nisha. For the first time in his life, he let someone love him—really love him. And now? Look at him. With his girls. Aidan? He gave up *everything*—his power, his position—just to be a father. Because Sonya showed him he deserved better."

I locked eyes with her, voice softer but no less fierce. "And me? Nobody gave a damn about me. I was groomed to take over after Aidan because nobody else would. I watched my brothers heal. I watched them build something real. And you—you're running away from it all."

"I'm trying to help you do the same thing. But you won't let anyone in. My family thinks you're trouble? Good. They thought the same thing about Nisha, about Sonya. I'm still choosing you. I'm still here. But you have to stop punishing me for trying to protect you."

And me?

Nobody gave a fuck about me.

"I was groomed to take after Aidan and I never wanted it after watching how Killian was treated. All three of us were abused since birth. Since the day we opened our eyes. You knew love. We had to guess!"

And now my heart ached, because this girl—this little thief—had no understanding for that.

"I endured, I suffered, I don't use it as an excuse to fuck up everyone else. My family thinks you are always going to choose yourself over everyone—so I choose *you* over everyone. Because I think better. I do. But if you don't choose me—"

She didn't wait for me to finish. She bolted out to her brother which I couldn't even be mad about.

Killian would've done the same.

28

VIVIANNE

Come to my dorm. Something happened with
Greenie.

ERIK'S TEXT CAME THROUGH, SHARP AND URGENT.

It had been three days since Kieran and I had exploded into that
fight—words thrown like knives, silence that felt like a chasm.

I was rushing out of the yoga studio, still slipping on my sneakers, heart pounding faster than my feet could carry me.

I ran faster than I ever had, catching a cab to his campus, my
heart threatening to burst through my chest.

The city streets became a chaotic maze.

The cab darted left, narrowly missing a cyclist, then swerved
right, the pursuing car relentless. Horns blared, tires screeched, and
the world shrank to a violent game of survival.

Not Erik. Please, not Erik.

But when I arrived, the door to Erik's apartment was ajar,
swinging slightly in the stale breeze.

My breath hitched. Inside, the scene was like a nightmare
bleeding into reality.

Erik stood frozen, his eyes wide and unblinking, locked on the
woman who had a gun pressed firmly against Greenie's side.

Greenie's face was forced down into the cold, unforgiving floor —his body trembling beneath the weight of the threat.

The woman's grip was unyielding, her every muscle taut with controlled fury.

Time slowed, the only sound the faint metallic click of the gun's safety being off.

My heart thundered in my chest, the room shrinking around me, trapping me in the raw terror of what could happen next.

"Hi," she smiled softly. And I recognized her from somewhere.

Oh.

Shit.

Fuck.

Kieran.

"*Reina?*" The word came out strangled.

Erik frowned, looking between us as teary-eyed Reina Lawless glared down at Greenie with barely contained rage.

"Vivianne, he tried to kill your brother."

"You know my sister?" Erik gaped, world tilting sideways. "You know her?"

"Yeah, that's Reina."

"What is she doing in your room?"

"She *was* my girlfriend."

"You were dating a Titan?"

"Umm, guys."

Reina pressed the gun harder into Greenie's back. "This motherfucker needs to be dealt with. Leo's on his way. You two need to get back."

Erik looked at Reina like a stranger.

The girl he'd told me made him feel normal wasn't who he thought she was. Just like Greenie wasn't who I thought he was.

My voice caught in my throat as I struggled to process it all.

"Reina Lawless is the operative you've been sleeping with?" The words felt foreign, harsh on my tongue. "Why didn't you tell me you were dating a Titan?"

"A Titan?" Erik blinked. "*What?*"

"Uhh, we might have some explaining to do."

2 9

KIERAN/ VIVIANNE

"You hired someone to sleep with my brother!"

Her voice shattered the silence—raw, accusing, trembling with a fury I'd seen only once before.

"He's a kid!"

I had expected this moment, dreaded it even, but hearing it out loud hit me like a blow I wasn't ready for.

"He's a fucking child, you played games with!"

She stood there—eyes blazing with disbelief, pain folding into rage—and it cut deeper than any bullet ever could.

And I didn't know what to say.

My hands clenched at my sides, fingers trembling as if they had a life of their own, weighted down by the truth she just spoke.

I wanted to reach for her, to pull her close and explain everything, but the words caught like thorns in my throat.

"It wasn't like that," I said finally, voice rough, ragged, barely holding myself together. "I did what I had to do...to protect him. To protect you."

But even as I spoke, I knew the words rang hollow.

Because this wasn't just anger she was feeling—it was something far deeper.

Betrayal. Loss. A fracture in something I feared might never heal.

And all I could do was stand there, vulnerable in the storm of her gaze, hoping she'd find a way to see beyond the damage.

She was betrayed. Not just by my actions, but by everything I represented—the cold calculations, the quiet manipulation, the impossible weight of secrets kept in shadows.

In her eyes, I was no longer the man she might have once trusted.

I had become a player in a ruthless game, one that used her family like chess pieces, pawns in a war she never asked to be part of.

Her gaze held a fierce, heartbreaking intensity—like a lantern searching through the darkness for a flicker of truth.

She was begging, silently pleading for me to be more than the monster she saw reflected back at her.

"I never wanted to hurt you," I whispered, my voice raw and trembling, breaking beneath the weight of my own confession. "I just…thought this was the only way."

But those words felt thin, fragile—like a fragile paper crane folded from lies and fear.

The silence stretched between us, thick and suffocating, folding time into an endless expanse.

The space was no longer just physical. It was the cavernous distance of broken trust, of wounds too fresh to heal.

Because sometimes, the very ones you long to shield from harm are the ones whose hearts you shatter most completely—without ever meaning to.

"I need to go to my family."

She stumbled, and I swore under my breath, the urge to protect her overwhelming as I scooped her up the best I could into my arms. Not picking her up, but corralling her into my side. And then hauling her to my room.

"Kiera—"

I didn't even let her finish.

She was so exhausted she let me.

In an instant, I had her pressed up against it, my emotions a swirling mix of anger, jealousy, and frustration, the intensity threatening to consume me.

My mouth pressed urgently against hers. Emotions running high as we frantically reached for each other.

"I need you." I rasped in a voice that didn't even sound like my own, my hands tugging impatiently at my pant.

"Need you—"

"I know—"

"Why did you run off?" I wrenched my shirt off over my head, flinging it aside as I pinned her again.

"You lied to me," she panted, still struggling with the fastenings of my pants.

"I didn't lie," I bit out, the words emerging breathless and ragged as I pulled her flush against me. "I just omitted the truth for my life. I would never hurt you."

"Yes, you would—" She was just as angry as I was.

And then I speared into her with one driving thrust, sheathing myself to the hilt in her welcoming heat. She gasped.

I wasn't gentle. I couldn't be.

I was as primal and ruthless as my intent as I arched and shoved deeper, swallowing her screams against my lips.

"Open for me."

I waited until she wrapped her arms around my neck and then I took her off the door and groaned as she sank lower on my cock.

Vivianne

I HAD TO TALK TO MY BROTHER ABOUT BEING A THIEF?

Perhaps.

But when I stood in front of him, the words I'd rehearsed a thousand times tangled in my throat and refused to come out.

The truth—the nights spent slipping through shadows, the cold thrill of stolen art, the endless mental chess game—felt too heavy to unload.

So I didn't say a word about any of it.

Instead, I chose simplicity.

"I work for Titan," I said, voice steady, eyes locked onto his like I was anchoring myself to something real, something safe.

No explanations.

No half-truths.

Just the barest truth that wouldn't shatter the fragile normalcy between us.

He nodded slowly, like the weight of my words settled over him like a warm balm. Relief softened his features, and I realized maybe this was all he needed for now. "That sounds...legit."

It wasn't the whole story. It wasn't the story he deserved. But it was enough—for now.

He hesitated, then asked quietly. "Are you going to be okay?"

I blew out a breath, the lie barely resting on my lips. "I am."

My brother was innocent—too pure for the world I inhabited, for the shadows I danced with.

He didn't know, and I wouldn't tell him. Not yet.

Because some truths weren't meant to be shared. Some secrets were better kept behind closed doors—safe, locked away, where they couldn't hurt the people you loved.

And for tonight, that was enough.

I messaged Gideon and Archer who were taking care of each of the Valentine's.

> Can you send her family a cut?

Already done. 40 mil. Per painting.

Done.

> And the Nash's?

Cleared.

Not a problem

> That's all I needed to hear

～

THE HOTEL LOBBY FELT COLDER THAN USUAL, OR MAYBE IT WAS JUST me—my chest tight, breath shallow, like the air itself was pressing down, holding me in place.

I gripped the handle of my suitcase, knuckles white, my mind racing with a thousand reasons to turn and walk away, to vanish before he saw me.

But then the air shifted—like a sudden crack in the silence—and his voice cut through the noise.

"Miss Valentine."

I looked up.

There *he* was.

Amber eyes. Dark oud. I would never forget how he smelled. I inhaled it into my lungs, expanding, contracting—and breathing harder with every step I took to him.

I couldn't think straight around him. But he didn't need to know that.

Mr. O'Hara—*Kieran*—stood just a few feet away, the weight of his presence folding over me like a storm waiting to break.

The space between us was heavy, charged with everything we hadn't said, everything we'd left unsaid.

Electric. Charged.

Uneasy.

That was always around me.

The air turned arid and cold and I wished to fucking God for once I had a better jacket. One I had bought.

His eyes caught mine, but they didn't have that usual sharp edge —the cold precision of a man used to holding everything tightly in his grasp.

No, they were softer. Raw. Haunted.

Like they carried the weight of every word he wanted to say but couldn't.

Like the silence between us was a wound neither of us dared touch.

"I didn't expect to see you here," he said, voice low, each word carefully measured, as if afraid to shatter the fragile thread holding us together.

Neither did I.

For a moment, neither of us moved. The noise of the lobby faded until all I could hear was the thundering of my own heart.

"Why now?" I finally whispered, the question trembling on my lips. "After everything."

He swallowed, and I saw the flicker of *something*—

Regret? Fear?

I looked down at my suitcase handle, the grip tight enough to hurt.

He took a slow step closer, the space between us shrinking, but still cautious, like he was testing the ground.

I met his gaze again, searching for the man behind the storm of control and anger—the man I thought I lost.

"Because I couldn't let you disappear without saying something."

FIVE YEARS LATER

KIERAN

THE SISTER-IN-LAWS WERE WILD.

Sonya, with her effortless elegance and laid-back charm, could hold her own with a mojito in hand—the kind of woman who made everything look easy.

But Lara and Nisha? Together, they were a force of nature.

Nisha's delighted squeals filled the room as Lara spun her around on the dance floor, their dresses shimmering in shades of pink and lilac, catching every light like they were made to dazzle.

They moved in perfect rhythm, like they'd known each other forever, unstoppable and alive.

The boys were on babysitting duty tonight.

Or rather, Alexei and—were on babysitting duty, leaving me to soak in the chaos and warmth of new friends.

Girlfriends.

Sonya laughed softly, slipping into the role of the responsible mom of the group as she pulled out her phone to text her husband.

I caught the moment and sent a video of Nisha and Lara gyrating, stealing the spotlight without a care, not even bothering to glance at my own phone afterward.

These two are so hot.

164

The night stretched on, full of laughter and the easy, electric connection of chosen family. I was home.

Sonya frowned over my shoulder as I took a slow sip, her eyes narrowing at the sight behind me.

Killian and Liam stood just a few feet away, and the moment the drink paused at my lips, a cold knot twisted in my stomach.

"Oh God."

Killian looked like the meanest motherfucker I'd ever seen—his jaw tight, eyes sharp as daggers.

He didn't waste a second on words. He cut a path straight to us, silent and fierce. Liam's voice was quieter, but urgent, demanding.

"Where's Lara?"

"Nisha?"

Sonya's gaze snapped to the dance floor, where Lara was swinging on a pole, her movements wild and uninhibited.

Nisha was close by, rolling her hips with a confidence that left no room for guessing.

Killian's breath hitched, his usual cold composure cracking just enough.

"I didn't know she could dance like that," he wheezed, a mix of disbelief and something protective flooding his tone.

Sonya's expression flickered—half amusement, half exasperation, like she didn't know whether to laugh or cry at the chaos unfolding.

I didn't fight the rising laughter that bubbled up as both men tore after their girls.

Liam reached Lara first, his arms outstretched, coaxing her down gently from the pole where she twirled recklessly.

Meanwhile, Nisha had already made her way halfway across the floor, dancing with another girl, hips swaying like she owned the night.

Killian caught her just in time, pulling her into his arms with a possessiveness that softened the rough edge in his eyes.

Sonya chuckled, shaking her head.

"I certainly hope the boys are entertained babysitting the kids instead of this," she said, voice warm and teasing.

I grinned, watching as Liam pulled Lara into a tight hug.

She pouted playfully, but the way her eyes sparkled told me she was happy. Nisha, on the other hand, looked like she was just grateful to be there, relaxed in Killian's arms.

And then he leaned in, capturing her mouth in a kiss that left no doubts.

"You guys are insane," I said, breathless and laughing.

"Says you," Sonya shot back with a grin.

She pulled out her phone, fingers flying over the screen. "Let me text Aidan. Crisis averted."

The guys took charge of getting us home, Liam behind the wheel, the city lights blurring past as we settled into the car.

In the backseat, Nisha was still wrapped up in Killian, their lips meeting in quiet moments between laughter.

Sonya had her arms around both Lara and me, anchoring us with her calm presence.

I found Vivianne on the mat Kiara sitting on her back and Marissa blowing bubbles on her face. The twins were playing with her hair braiding it with flowers or something.

I smirked.

"Girls? Did you guys pounce on my lady?"

All six eyes bat up at me.

"No," Marissa waved her wand. "Boo!"

I grinned wider as Killian behind me moved to pick her up.

"Come on, Mari, Daddy wants some snuggles and gnocchi."

For the first time in a long time, I felt the pulse of family—not perfect, loud, messy, and fiercely protective—and I wanted to hold onto that feeling forever.

DE-BRIEF

Thank you so much for joining the O'Hara's on adventures in the Underworld Kings.

I cannot wait for you to meet the Midnight Gods

Lilah

EXCERPT FROM STROKE OF LUCK

CHAPTER ONE

I was going to throw my drink at the sleazy Suit and Tie with a cocky smirk, his wedding ring glinting under the club lights.

"Let me take you home tonight."

Biting back a comment, I tried not to let it grate on my nerves that it was because of men like Suit and Tie over here that I was bringing in my twenty-fifth birthday today, a virgin.

Instead of blaming it on life, a tiny dating pool filled with arse-holes, and the responsibilities that consumed me?

My frustrations were on this idiot.

I had come to Teasers, one of New York's premier burlesque clubs, intending to escape.

Around me, the 1920's style decor, with floating multi-colored parasol umbrellas and lush, warm lighting, created a wonderland for seduction.

Scantily-clad performers in colorful wings, lingerie meant to be torn off with guests, and feather boas wrapped around their necks —I would have been in girl heaven.

The scent of white sage and flowers from the live plants mingled in the air, usually a comfort—now tainted by Suit and Tie's cheap cologne. Fidgeting with the vines dangling near my shoulder, I leaned back against the plush velvet barstool, trying to maintain distance.

"No, thank you," I replied firmly, but his eyes only widened, his smirk growing.

"Goddamn, your accent is sexy," he was undeterred.

"I'm waiting for someone." *Anyone. But you.*

As he reached out, I scooted further back, but before I could react, a figure in black obstructed my view.

The unmistakable scent of sea and spice filled my senses, and for a moment, I shifted in my seat, my heart pounding.

Reed Whittaker, CEO of Titan Security and the source of all my sexual frustration for the last three years, blocked my view. Broad shoulders. Chocolate hair.

The kind of look that made a woman think twice about her late-night decisions.

"Not gonna happen," Reed rumbled, his rich, velvety baritone laced with quiet menace.

The Suit and Tie sounded offended, his bravado deflating. "Who the fuck are you?"

"Don't even think about it," Reed said in a voice I heard over the music. "Turn around, go back to your friends."

Reed cut an intimidatingly rugged figure even among the common masses, exuding an undercurrent of raw power usually reserved for archangels strolling among humans.

The aura of intensity radiated from him.

Reed liked to make the occasional unannounced visit to Teasers, and by some stroke of luck, I seemed to be there on those nights.

His focus remained fixed on me the nights he was here, ensuring my safety even when I hadn't realized I needed protection.

But I figured that was his job. I told myself it wasn't a big deal. He'd usher me into cabs, steadying me with those large, calloused hands.

Except for that one night months ago when a friend's early departure prompted my exit shortly after.

As I approached the entrance, Reed materialized from the shadows.

Is everything all right? Is there anyone taking you home?...I can.

Why? I can catch a cab...

I just want to make sure you get home safe. Can I do that?

Sure...

Reed walked me to my doorstep, remaining in the hall until I was safely inside.

The entire interaction burned itself into my consciousness. Just a man ensuring a woman's safe passage home. Even though I hadn't so much as touched a drop at the club that night, the memory alone intoxicated me for weeks afterward.

He wanted to make sure I was safe. Without touching me. He never pushed for more.

Almost like he waited until I was comfortable.

A warm heat blossomed within me that had nothing to do with filling any empty space. Just his mere existence was enough to set me alight.

Because I wanted Reed. Lara confided that she trusted him implicitly to protect everyone.

Reed took that responsibility seriously.

I didn't hear what Suit and Tie said to Reed.

He was sputtering before Reed, and even surrounded by the dancers, every eye around me in the club seemed inexplicably drawn to this. Suit and Tie grumbled something under his breath.

The taut line of Reed's shoulders tensed like he was physically restraining himself.

"I'm not going to repeat myself. Get out. Or you can get kicked out."

"Yeah, and who the fuck are you?"

I saw the way Reed's entire body stiffened. *Drat.*

Before I could overthink it, I reacted on sheer instinct. I don't know what possessed me then, but I felt the dangerous shift as Reed tipped his head, his body coiling.

On instinct, I reached out, and my hand found its way into his. "Reed."

The instant we made contact, he looked over his shoulder at me, those storm-cloud eyes flashing with an untamed intensity that stole my breath.

I shook my head slightly, silently pleading. Unspeakable emotions lingered in his gaze as it raked over me with heat.

I injected some tease into my voice. "Where have you been? I've been waiting for you." *In more ways than one.*

His brow furrowed a fraction, and I willed him with my eyes to just go along with it.

Please, just play along. He searched my face intently.

When his head swung back towards the hapless suit, Reed was every inch the merciless predator, catching the attention of the rest of the club's security.

One of them, Nate Wyatt, a blonde Viking of a man, emerged soundlessly to stand at Reed's side.

Unlike Reed, Nate wore a shirt that said "Security" on the back.

Though not as massively built as Reed's, Nate's broad shoulders and navy eyes radiated an equal aura of threat.

He took one look at the slime ball, not hesitating in the slightest to reach out and lift him bodily from his seat.

I was too stunned to speak, unconsciously gripping Reed's hand.

A silent look passed between Nate and Reed, and whatever he saw in his boss's eyes made Nate shake his head at the suit, almost sympathetically.

I held my breath as the man squawked indignantly about harassment and lawsuits.

Nate all but growled, flanked by two other immense security guards, forcibly ejecting not just Suit and Tie, but his entire friend group. All because of me.

Embarrassment flooded me as I tried to tug my hand back from Reed's grip.

But he wouldn't release me, as his eyes followed his men until they disappeared from view, seemingly oblivious to the murmuring crowd we had attracted.

Reed loosened his grip, though his fingers remained tangled with mine.

"Don't feel bad," he said evenly, as though dealing with such confrontations was all in a night's work for him.

Tousled chocolate hair, just messy enough to tempt wandering fingers. A jawline perpetually tense.

Clean-shaven and smelling like the sea, Reed Whittaker was the kind of man who made women rethink their decisions. Several times.

He towered over my frame, forcing me to tip my head back to meet that stormy gaze head-on from where I sat.

Reed fit the dark, seductive aesthetic of the club like he was born to it.

He ran Teasers security with an iron fist, yet he moved through the crowd with an ease, a comfort of knowing he was in charge.

Everyone yielded to him.

He didn't dress the part of a CEO, his classic bomber jacket over a white shirt.

Powerfully built, the loose material hinted at the sinewy muscles beneath.

My imagination ran wild with visions of him making love to me beneath the cascading waterfall installation or near the canopy of pink cherry blossoms draped over the mezzanine.

He made me feel a little unhinged, untamed.

A little out of it.

Growing up with a Bengali-English mother and an English father, my baby sister Avani and I had inherited a blend of mannerisms and cultural practices from our parents.

Once, I landed in Reed's arms when I nearly took a spill months ago.

Reed had materialized by my side with lightning-fast reflexes, one broad palm across the small of my back, catching me against his solid chest before I could fall.

I still remember covering my burning face with a hand and murmuring an embarrassed thanks, unconsciously dipping into a tiny, deferential bow of gratitude.

A habit ingrained from my Mum.

When I finally peeked up at him through my lashes, Reed's lips curved into an amused smile that set my olive skin ablaze with a crimson flush.

My friends loved to tease me about my not-so-subtle fixation on Reed, which I staunchly denied.

After all, I had an obligation to Avani to not parade a revolving cast of potential lovers before her.

To my sister, I was already unconventional as a pseudo-parent.

Being a successful social media influencer, I'd been so focused on raising Avani and running my business that I neglected my own needs and desires.

Dating was one realm of life I had no experience navigating. Men were a no-go.

The influencer life was less glamorous than people thought, and it had left me feeling emptier than I wanted to feel. Which led me to Teasers tonight. Desperate to no longer feel so stuck.

Privately dreaming of Reed showing me what I'd been missing. Wondering if the reality could possibly live up to the fantasies.

"Are you all right?" The rough timbre of Reed's voice dragged me from my wandering thoughts.

That familiar clench of his jaw, the storm brewing in his eyes.

It paralyzed me every time our paths crossed.

I had barely exchanged words with him, yet the charged silence crackled, threatening to consume me if he so much as brushed against me.

I blamed it on the pent-up energy and not because Reed was well...Reed.

"You didn't have to do all that," I managed, shaking my head minutely. "I didn't want to make a scene."

"You didn't make a scene," Reed's deep voice washed over me as he stated the obvious with maddening calm. "I did."

Reed was a looming storm.

The stillness before the lightning cracked through the sky. I told myself the fluttering in my ribcage was simply the effects of too many mojitos consumed too quickly on an empty stomach.

"Does that happen to you often?"

It did. More than he knew.

The overzealous fans at meet and greets. The creepy comments on my Instagram and social media in general.

Pinned by the weight of his stare, I didn't know how to answer him. Something lurked under his surface, something that told me he hadn't stopped thinking about what he'd like to do to Suit and Tie.

"It's all right."

174

"It's not alright. He shouldn't have tried to put his hands on you," Reed's eyes darkened as he bit out the words. He raked over the slinky dress, hugging my curves before snagging on my heels.

"He didn't—"

"He was going to," Reed stated. "That was enough."

"Enough?" I repeated.

Reed's face remained impassive. "Why did you hold me back?" Storm cloud eyes took me in.

"I don't want you getting into a fight."

Over me. Even I didn't have enough ego to voice it.

Reed's eyes intensified as though confused.

"I don't like the idea of...people getting hurt over..." *Oh, drat, I am floundering.* "I don't want you to get hurt over something so..."

Seeing me struggle, Reed leaned in, halting my rambling. "You don't want me to fight for you?"

Did he want to fight?

I couldn't think with him this close. I had the biggest crush on Reed.

"Why would you?" I managed to whisper.

His brows rose fractionally as though incredulous I'd even ask such a thing.

I could only murmur. "I don't understand. I just didn't want to see you hurt."

Something unguarded flickered in Reed's eyes as they softened momentarily. He clearly hadn't expected that response. His hand shifted to cup the side of my neck, thumb brushing the dangle of my earring.

A hint of wry amusement filled his expression, though he found my concern for his well-being laughable.

"What are you doing here tonight?"

I lifted my chin at his censuring tone, taking in the press of his full lips, drawing into a slight frown, brows furrowed. How did I even begin to answer that?

"You haven't been here in a while," Reed murmured.

I want to get laid.

Preferably by a man who looks and smells like you. Do you have a brother?

175

I deflected. "A girl's not allowed to have a drink and enjoy her Friday night?" *Or her birthday.*

His head tipped in that subtle way that really shouldn't have looked effortless. "It's Sunday."

Drat. His hand fell from my neck to brace against the back of the chair, and I immediately missed the contact.

Keeping track of the date often proved challenging in my unconventional lifestyle—the not-so-glamorous hustle of an influencer rarely adhered to regular business hours or anything resembling a routine.

He dipped his head, brushing my ear.

"How much have you had to drink?"

I clenched my thighs instinctively, my palm lifting to press against the firm wall of his jacketed chest. Instead of pushing him away, I seemed to anchor myself to his solid presence.

"I'm fine, I just—"

"How much?" His dubious expression made it clear he didn't believe me for a second.

Avoiding his searing stare, I glanced toward the remnants of my drinks. "Three?"

Reed's mouth ticked up at the corners, a rueful amusement dancing in his eyes.

"If you plan on staying here all night, lightweight, you'll have me for company."

My eyes widened, bristling at the gentle jab as a frisson of heated awareness licked through me at the implication of him staying by my side all night.

"Lightweight?" I echoed, indignant.

Reed grinned, his tongue darting out a little between his teeth as he leaned against the bar top.

"You're like Bambi on ice when you drink," he murmured, eyes dancing with mirth. I could only see his tongue and felt my entire body respond to that.

I could hear my governess in my head. Ladies do not daydream of being taken like a wild woman by a man like this.

I gasped, affronted. "I'm appalled by your candor. I can absolutely hold my weight—"

"Even when you're offended, you're still so..." His achingly sensual smile only widened as I sputtered.

"Articulate?" I supplied, arching a brow.

"Proper," Reed countered, that Northeastern accent rendering the simple word into something indecently sensual as it rolled off his tongue.

A weighted beat stretched between us, the air thrumming with unvoiced tension. Reed's gaze seemed to search my face, his brow furrowing slightly as if piecing together a puzzle.

"How long did your family move you guys around?" he asked abruptly. "Kids usually have accents if they've been around another language until about thirteen or so."

I blinked, startled by his astute observation.

Memories of my childhood flashed through my mind.

The familiar streets of Chiswick, the rolling hills of Oxfordshire, occasional stints in America, and trips to Calcutta, which my parents took us on to preserve Mum's culture. My Mum's voice echoed in my ears, her soft accent a constant backdrop to our lives. A life I no longer had.

"I was a teenager..."

Reed nodded, his eyes never leaving mine. It was as if he was absorbing the information, tucking it away for future reference.

Reed tipped his head back, looking behind me, his eyes darkening.

"Are you going to do that cute little bow again when you thank me for saving you this time?"

My heart stuttered at the word "cute".

I fought to keep my composure, willing myself not to visibly react.

Do not combust. Do not move.

As his words fully registered, confusion swept through me." Save me from what?"

EXCERPT FROM LEGACY

CHAPTER ONE

"Motherfucker."

Running across a rooftop at midnight to catch a criminal was not the way I wanted my Friday night to go down. Not exactly.

I was going to kill this motherfucker.

I leapt off the building I was in, the wind whipping in my hair, as I gained on the fucker running from me.

The skyline around me stretched out the lights guiding me towards my target. A maze of concrete that I knew would hurt if I splattered on it.

Street pizza was not what I wanted to be tonight.

Not when I was chasing a potential perp.

God, when I got my fucking claws and fangs into him—he'd scream for a completely different reason.

I was bolting down and right before he hit the next building, I caught him at the edge.

"Not so fast, fucker." It was a growl ripped from my throat as he elbowed me. With a snarl I had him on the ground. But he was a fighter.

He maneuvered in a way that I felt the elbow coming at my throat and ducked, landing on my back.

He took off, leaping over the edge. I shouted as I drew back and took the jump with him.

I thought he'd make it.

He kinda did, but he groaned as he hit the ground. I definitely made it the air whooshing from my lungs as I rolled smoothly.

Or I would've. I landed wrong.

I felt a searing pain in my shoulder that ripped right through me as I groaned. But my other hand moved. My gun yanking out as I took the shot.

With confidence. He groaned going down as I saw him get hit.

"Fuck!" I groaned dropping onto my knees. I shot him again taking him out as I heard someone land next to me.

"Boss, you good?"

Landon Donohue.

My right hand most of the time when I was working.

I looked up into dark eyes and darker hair whipping in the wind as another man dropped down next to him.

Derek Macall, shaved head, piercings and tattoos. My team. Sean was downstairs in the car.

I let out a breath.

"Straight." I would get Kieran to set it.

Three days later, Kieran did not in fact set it and the pain was getting too excruciating to ignore.

I couldn't. But I didn't wanna go to the hospital and deal with another presumptuous doctor or nurse ever again. But I couldn't stop myself.

Sean watched me one evening struggling to put my jacket on.

"Just ask for Nisha Graham when you go," he muttered. His clear blue eyes watched me wincing a little. "She's solid. Nicest lady there."

"Just because you got favorites, doesn't mean I trust them." I bit out. "You fuck her or something?"

He made a noise. "Nah, she's cool." Right. He just looked uneasy as I groaned about my shoulder. "Just go check it out tonight."

"Fine. I'll go."

"Nisha Graham." Sean repeated. "Trust me. She's good."

We'll see about that.

~

A cat photo from Kieran lit up my phone screen on the way to the hospital with Nisha.

It was of a chubby gray cat with a bandaged paw, frowning at the camera.

> That's you.

Another photo appeared of a regal black cat with a crown rolling its eyes.

> That's big bro.

I snorted.
I sent him back a photo of a tombstone.

> Keep texting me annoying shit and this will be you.

> BWahahah. Nice to see you getting on board the meme train.

> Such a fucking idiot

> You didn't fix my arm

> I'm not a doctor

> That was your first mistake with me

I groaned.
Little brother's fucking sucked sometimes.
Even if I loved the little shit.
Right now, my shoulder throbbing in pain?
I couldn't focus on anything else.

> Such a shit

> Go to the hospital, bro

COMING SOON

AN EXCERPT FROM THE HUNTER

Andrei DuPont & Talia Nash

THE HUNTER

TALIA

"Andrei!"

I squealed as I bolted through the woods behind campus.

Nobody was going to come bother us at Saints Academy out here. Especially not on the first night back when everyone was getting settled in.

Masculine laughter filled the area around me as birds flew wildly over my head. The twigs snapped under my feet as I pumped my arms.

I was delighted.

"You won't catch me!" I cried.

"We'll see about that!"

I could feel the sweat beading on the back of my neck as I leapt over fallen logs, branches, twigs, and I kept going laughter coming from me as I did.

No way he's going to catch me.

Being chased by my boyfriend of over seven years was one way to celebrate Halloween. But I trusted Andrei with my life. I always had.

And if he caught me?

Shivers crept down my neck at the thought of that.

A sharp breaking sound came from behind me and I let out an eep as I heard his delighted chuckle.

Dark and sinfully sexy, Andrei was approaching and I didn't even want to look back knowing it was so deep in twilight that I wouldn't make it.

Even if I was prey, I wasn't an idiot.

And maybe this particular prey wanted to be devoured.

I could swear I felt his breath behind me before I could even process it, I was tackled from behind, and a scream left me.

I trust him, I trust him, I trust him.

I told myself that as we went crashing down together into the dirt and grass and another muffled scream left me as Andrei took the brunt of it.

A groan left him.

"Are you all right, mon coeur?" He groaned. His *heart*.

That's what he called me.

I must've made a noise or something because Andrei's hands were checking my head, making sure I was good and I was face to face with the most beautiful man I'd ever seen in my entire life.

Galaxy brown-eyes rimmed with a black ring around the pupil in the prettiest shade of blue on Earth watched me with amusement and concern mingling in them.

His cut cheekbones, clean-shaved face, and tapered hair cut only brought out he was too pretty to even be real.

Andrei Alexandre DuPont was *mine*.

"Are you all right?"

I nodded feeling breathless as my chest heaved. "This doesn't mean you won. You probably cheated."

His grin was wide, canines flashing and his eyes twinkling all alien blue. "Say what you want, mon coeur I won." His lips dipped over mine. "And now I get whatever I want."

His lips stamped over mine and I knew exactly what he wanted.

Shamelessly, I was soaked for him as I felt his fingers yanking at my skirt. Ripping my panties and stocking down the middle and I felt his fingers on my clit.

"Drew," I panted. "I'm spotting a little."

"You already know I don't care," he muttered before thrusting his tongue into my mouth making me suck. And I felt the energy shifting as the sun was going down around me.

"Drew—"

"I gotcha," he growled. And I moaned for another reason when I felt his broad head pushing against the entrance of my pussy. "Fucckk."

"I need—"

He stamped his mouth over mine and kept it there as he pumped himself into my soaking wet body. A muffled scream erupted as I felt stretched out in the brutal thrusts he laid into me.

Strangled cries left my throat muffled with his mouth and the slight sting of pain of me adjusting was familiar.

A muffled noise left me as he let my mouth go.

"Shhh, mon ange, I have you," he whispered, voice thick with lust. "I *always* have you."

A rush of heat spread through my body at the way he sank deeper, and I lost my train of thought. It spread through my body like a full blown attack, every nerve in me blazing with electric sensations.

My heart was going to implode if he kept this up.

Another noise left me as Andrei rocked his hips into me until he bottomed out.

"Oh God," my moan was low. His kisses wrecked me. Rough and hot. Explosive to the touch. I loved this man. "Please fuck me."

"I knew you'd be soaking for me," the eerie shade of blue was back in my vision while he was taking up every single inch of space he could. "But hearing you beg is something else entirely."

His tongue darted out licking a path down my throat, the sensitive column where my pulse pounded in time to the way he throbbed in me.

Nothing was more intimate than this.

Outside, where anyone could find us. Where the world would know Andrei DuPont was my lover. His hands roamed over my body tearing up my sweater. Yanking it until my breasts heaved and the first flick of his tongue on my nipples I was shaking.

"*Drew.*"

He hummed as he drew out of me and I felt every single pulsating inch.

A jolt of pleasure went through me at the first brutal thrust into me. Sometimes I forgot how strong he was, muscles bunched under my fingertips.

Andrei drove into me with a series of effortlessly vicious thrusts that left me a mess.

My cries echoing in the woods as the trees above me shadowed us. His teeth sank into a nipple and I felt the pleasure crest so fast— I exploded.

As I did, he rose above me like a ruthless god more than man, Andrei propped my leg on one shoulder as his drives began hitting somewhere sweeter.

I sobbed as the pressure rose as I came. He didn't relent.

He didn't let me calm down.

Instead he drove so deep in me I lost my breath and held onto the ground, my fingers trying desperately to catch onto something as he fucked.

This was where I found peace. Andrei was my soul. Around everyone else we wrestled with whatever they wanted us to be. Perfect little cartoon images of our true selves. But here?

Where we were one? Nothing but man and woman?

I reveled in what he did to me.

He lifted my other leg onto his shoulder and began driving into me at an angle that made me scream.

"That's it, scream for me, say my fucking name."

"*Drew.*"

"You can be as loud as you want out here for me, mon coeur," he growled as thrust after thrust made me lose it. "Let them hear you being fucked like an animal."

I shrieked as I came from that alone.

"That's." *Thrust.* "My." *Thrust.* "Fucking." *Thrust.* "Girl."

I was dying.

"You love me destroying this tight little pussy, don't you?"

"Oh God," I squealed as my orgasm became unrelenting.

It was white hot. Dangerous. Every inch of me felt obliterated leaving behind nothing but mind numbing pleasure.

Insanely, dimly, I was aware of myself shrieking so loud Andrei lowered his body folding me in half and I forgot how to breathe.

One orgasm after another wracked through me.

"My girl liked being hunted and fucked, didn't she?"

"Y-yes."

Tremors wracked through me as he groaned. "Come for me, one more time, mon coeur."

"Drew—"

"Now."

My back would've bowed had he not slammed his length into me lighting me up from the inside out. In the kind of orgasm that seemed to come from somewhere deeper than before.

An animal noise left me as I came on his command.

I couldn't breathe, couldn't process anything until I felt his heat flooding me, the length of him swelling before he buried deep.

A long satisfied groan left him as he dropped my legs and sealed his mouth over mine grinding so deep in me I saw stars.

I couldn't stop shaking as he kissed me quiet.

Andrei was always like this. More animal than man. More mine than his own.

My entire soul in one person who I loved and trusted beyond anything else in the world.

Noises left me as I calmed down and felt the aftershocks racing through me. As he kissed me, I calmed down.

"You are my entire life, Talia," he murmured over my lips. "I'm not letting anything happen to you."

ABOUT THE AUTHOR

Lilah Lance writes romance for all the girls who dream of being seen, being *accepted*, and being loved for *who they are.*

Get exclusive content and giveaways by signing up for Lilah's newsletter on http://lilahlance.com where you can get sneak peeks and news before anyone else.